W9-AMN-593

THE LEGEND OF
STOREY COUNTY

A NOVEL

THE LEGEND OF STOREY COUNTY

A NOVEL

BROCK THOENE

THOMAS NELSON PUBLISHERS
Nashville • Atlanta • London • Vancouver

Published in association with the literary agency of:

Alive Communications, Inc.
P.O. Box 49068
Colorado Springs, CO 80949

Published in Nashville, Tennessee, by Jan Dennis Books, an imprint
of Thomas Nelson, Inc., Publishers, and distributed in Canada by
Word Communications, Ltd., Richmond, British Columbia.

Library of Congress Cataloging-in-Publication Data

Thoene, Brock, 1952–
    The legend of Storey County / Brock Thoene.
      p.   cm.
    "A Jan Dennis book."
    ISBN 0-7852-8070-7
    1. Frontier and pioneer life—Sierra Nevada (Calif. and Nev.)—
Fiction. 2. Storey County (Nev.)—History—Fiction. 3. United
States—History—Civil War, 1861–1865—Fiction. 4. Twain,
Mark, 1835–1910—Fiction. I. Title.
PS3570.H463L4   1995
813'.54—dc20   95–16382
                                        CIP

Printed in the United States of America
1 2 3 4 5 6 — 00 99 98 97 96 95

DEDICATION

This story is for Mom,
with love.

PROLOGUE

The Last Run of the V&T Railroad
Carson City to Virginia City, Nevada
September 27, 1938

The chuffing steam engine of the Silver Short Line was decked out in red, white, and blue bunting borrowed from the Virginia City Masonic Lodge's Fourth of July decorations box.

"Don't know why they've dressed the old girl up like she's going to a party." The ancient conductor's voice quaked. He squinted out the window at the Volunteer Firemen's brass band as it played an off-key medley of Sousa marches. Pale blue eyes were nearly hidden beneath folds of skin and grizzled eyebrows, and his leathery face seemed like a topographical map of the desert. "Ain't no celebration. It's a funeral, that's what. Should've dressed her in mourning. All in black. In black, I say!" He jerked his gnarled thumb at the black armband on his sleeve. "They oughta be playin' 'Death's Harvest Time'! That's what."

Eyes heavenward, the conductor hummed a refrain of the morbid hymn. With tremulous flourish, he punched the ticket of the sandy-haired, studious young man in the rumpled brown suit who sat in the back of the train car with a half dozen other passengers.

Seth Townsend, reporter for the *San Francisco Examiner,* had been sent to write the obituary of the Virginia and Truckee Silver Short Line as she made her final run from Carson City to Virginia City, Nevada. From the sparse company of travelers, Townsend surmised that there was not much interest in the event. But somebody at the *Examiner* thought it was historical, human-interest type material, and who was Townsend to argue with a three-day journey and an expense account? Never mind that the trip was plagued by the searing temperatures of the hottest summer in Nevada history. Never mind that his expense account was barely enough to pay for a sagging bed in a squalid brick rooming house with a window opening onto the belching smoke of the train yard. This was Townsend's first assignment out of the Bay Area. He was determined that he would bring back a story even if he had to make one up.

Careful to maintain a respectful expression, Townsend flipped open his notebook and wagged his head in mock sorrow at the demise of the steam train.

"'Death's Harvest Time'?" Townsend's gray eyes followed the conductor's gaze to the water-stained passenger car ceiling as though he were trying to recall the lyrics of the song. He sighed heavily as if struck through with the tragedy of the occasion. It was best not to mention that he was being paid five cents per column inch for the article. Bad poetry could certainly take up at least an inch and a half in an *Examiner* column. Quoting a hymn was easy money.

"'Death's Harvest Time.'" Townsend tapped his forehead. "It's right here . . . Lemme see . . . something, *something,* something . . . *Death's Harvest* . . . something?"

The conductor, who smelled of stale whiskey and old tobacco smoke, blinked suspiciously down at the shorthand scribbles in Townsend's notebook and then fixed his eyes on the bulky Speed Graphic news camera on the seat beside Townsend.

"You some kind of newspaper wag or something? Newspapers down here in Carson have been all for progress. All for shutting down the V&T . . ."

"Not a bit of it. San Francisco boy. Come to pay my respects, that's all. Take a picture to hand down to my kids . . . if I ever have kids. Historic day. Last run and all. The V&T Railroad and Virginia City mines together is what built San Francisco they say. I wanted to have a look." This was said with a mixture of sincerity and innocence that caused the old conductor to believe he had found a kindred spirit in this callow youth and that perhaps not every young person was going to the dogs after all.

"True enough!" He roared his approval and added instruction. "Take a good long look. The end of the V&T means the end of Virginia City! The end of the city that built San Francisco. All those Nob Hill millionaires? They all got their start grubbing in the dust of Mount Davidson! Up there through Six Mile Canyon. All of 'em. Name any of the big society fellas in San Francisco! No better than

you or me. Just lucky, that's all! Don't forget it either. They
struck it rich at the end of the line! The Comstock. No
place like it in the world. Never was before. Never will be
again! Like the mines of King Solomon only richer. And
my! How they all lived like kings. Forgot where they come
from. Forgot you and me and the V&T too." The conductor's faded blue eyes clouded with memories. He hovered
over Townsend in silence and smiled wistfully as if he could
see some pleasant image in the distance. The shrill wail of
the train whistle pulled his thoughts back to the present.
"Well. They ain't worth anything now! Bones and dust.
Worth less than those heaps of yellow mine tailings they left
all over them hills. All that fuss. Now they ain't anything
but slag heaps with fancy headstones. And what's it for in
the end?"

"Guess you saw it all? The silver boom? Mother lode
tycoons." Townsend touched the pencil lead to his tongue,
ready for the story.

"I'm only seventy-seven, a sprout." The conductor dis-
missed Townsend's flattery, which implied he was the best
choice to deliver the eulogy for so venerable a pair of corpses
as the V&T and Virginia City.

"Lots of memories?" Townsend's pencil poised over the
paper.

"Only enough for my life. You're a few years late, young
fella. There's only one left who saw it from the beginning.
Old Jim. Oldest man in Storey County. But he don't like
strangers much. The real boom was over when I come
along." He shrugged and changed the subject. "But you've
got the words to 'Death's Harvest Time' all wrong."

"My mother's favorite hymn."

The band bleated Sousa's "Stars and Stripes Forever" as the conductor carefully dictated the lyrics to the funeral dirge for the Virginia and Truckee Silver Short Line Railroad.

> *I saw Death come in the Springtime*
> *And enter a lovelit bower,*
> *Where from the breast of a mother,*
> *He gathered a fair young flower.*
> *I said to Him, "Death, what doest thou here?"*
> *"My harvest," said He, "lasteth all the year."*

Mentally calculating seven and a half cents for verse one, Townsend wiped a feigned tear from his eye, murmured his thanks, and said something about the true heartfelt beauty of great old songs as the conductor shuffled away through the car.

———◦•◦•◦———

The hike up to Virginia City's C Street from the V&T train station was tiring enough. It was more like mountain climbing than walking. Townsend stopped on the uneven planks of the boardwalk, pulled a white handkerchief from his pocket, and mopped his forehead and his neck. Below his chin, his throat prickled along the line where his scraggly beard ended.

Ducking under the awning, Townsend paused in the shade. Maybe chasing after some old coot was a bad idea. Hiking around the windblown remains of a semianimated ghost town in one hundred and ten degrees was seeming less and less like a good plan.

The reporter wiped the cloth across his face once more and noted that it came away stained with pale red dust. He snorted as the pun crossed his mind that maybe this was what his editor had meant about "soaking up the local color." Maybe he could just load up his story with phrases like "once glorious past," and "proud achievements of the pioneers." That should do the trick. Then add a few photos of the ancient relic of a train and that would be that.

Almost against his will, he thought that the story would be improved if he could find some old photos of the town in its heyday—steam engine and cars shiny and new, a company of volunteer firemen marching to the train platform before a Fourth of July picnic—something that suggested a present, instead of just a long-forgotten past.

The sign over the door of the red brick building against which Townsend leaned proclaimed that the premises were occupied by the *Territorial Enterprise*. A newspaper office! Some vague memory stirred in the newsman's head, a single answer on a USC multiple choice exam in history of journalism. But what had been the question?

The place looked deserted. A window shade, broken loose from its mooring, slanted limply across cracked panes. The faded and warped wooden panels testified that the building was not in use, yet the door was ajar.

Townsend poked his head into the dusty interior but heard nothing. He rapped on the door with his knuckles and called out, then succumbed to a fit of sneezing brought on by the dust dislodged by his knock.

"Yeah? Wha'da you want?" growled a voice. A short, bald-headed man emerged from the gloom. From his round face protruded an unlit cigar stub.

"Is this the office of the *Territorial Enterprise?*" Townsend inquired.

"Used to be," the stubby figure affirmed. "Been out of business ten years already."

The reporter was disappointed. "Sorry I bothered you then," he said. "I'm with the *Examiner,* covering the last run of the V&T. Thought maybe I could find some old photos to go with my story."

"Yeah?" The cigar stayed firmly clenched between the pudgy lips, but the growl took on a note of interest. "Good idea, but too late. Most of the files burnt up years ago. The rest . . . I dunno. Blake's my name. I used to work here in the twenties."

Townsend was still trying to recall why this little flyspeck of a paper should have been on a college exam. "Did anybody famous ever work here?" he said.

"Plenty!" was the emphatic reply. "Did you ever hear of Joe Goodman?"

Townsend shook his head.

"Dan DeQuille? Rollin Daggett? Real, rip-sawing newspapermen. Not like today's sniveling pen pushers."

Townsend shook his head again and received a heavy sigh in return. "I suppose it was too much to hope for. All right . . . you have heard of Mark Twain, I hope?"

The reporter from the *Examiner* snapped his fingers. "That's it! Twain was here."

"Got his start here!" Blake roared. "Never was a good newspaperman. Too busy making up lies to bother with digging for the truth!"

The connection pleased Townsend. He would figure out some way to work Mark Twain into his tribute; give the piece a literary bent. "Well, thanks for the information," he said, turning to leave.

"S'pose you'll be writing about Twain now," Blake grumbled. "Well, at least you can still get the truth about that!"

Townsend stopped in his tracks. "What do you mean?"

"Old Jim Canfield, who lives up on the corner of Howard and King. He can tell you stories about Twain."

This had to be the same man the conductor had mentioned. "He was here? With Mark Twain? This man knew Twain personally?"

"What have I been talkin' here, Swahili? Course he knew Twain. Are you a reporter or not? Go see the man! Ask him."

───•◦•◦•───

The hill from the center of town up to Howard Street was every bit as steep as the climb from the train station to the *Territorial Enterprise*. Puffing and panting, Townsend composed a sentence about how Virginia City perched on the shoulder of Mount Davidson like a . . . like a what? A fly? A crow? What would Twain have said?

The little house located at the end of Blake's directions was faded blue, much the same color as the pale sky overhead. It was tired looking and in need of paint. The tin roof was dull and streaked down from the rusting stovepipes that protruded through the steep pitched metal.

The back porch leaned out over a yard that dropped away beneath it in miniature imitation of the way the whole town clung to the hillside. The structure sagged in the middle.

In the corner between the porch and the house sat an occupied rocking chair. Each creak of the chair was replied to by a squawk from the floorboards. Townsend peered into the shade, but the contrast between the glare of the sun and the shadow prevented him from being able to make out the features of the occupant, except for a glimpse of white hair.

As the reporter leaned over the short picket fence and shielded his eyes from the sun, a voice called out to him from the porch, "You looking for me?" It was a deep tone, husky with age. A dignified rumble to clear the throat followed his question.

"Excuse me," Townsend said. "Are you old Jim, I mean, Mister Jim Canfield?"

"Reckon so. Been that for most of a hundred years. You came to talk to me, right?"

"Yessir. How did you know?"

"Ain't nobody gonna climb this hill in the midday heat, 'less they're coming on purpose to see somebody. Everybody else is down to the train station doings, 'cept me. So, you must be coming to see me. Come on in."

Townsend swung open the gate into the garden, then ascended a narrow flight of wooden steps to the porch. Once on the planks, his eyes adjusted to the light and he studied the man seated in the rocking chair.

The face that regarded him from below white hair slightly yellowed with age was a deep tan. Down the dark face coursed creases and wrinkles, like those found across the toe of a well-broken-in leather shoe.

The hands that gripped the knobby ends of the rocker arms were themselves knobby with age, knuckles protruding as if the muscles of once powerful hands had shrunk away from the bone.

Everything about Jim Canfield spoke of immense age, and Townsend began to believe that the stooped figure really was that of a man one hundred years old. But could the memory of one so ancient be relied on?

The issue was settled when the reporter looked into Canfield's eyes and found a steady gaze studying him with amusement. Embarrassed, Townsend peered through the back window of the cabin, pretending to examine a row of photographs lined up on a shelf inside the small parlor. "Know what you're thinking." Canfield said. "Still got all my marbles. Now ask your question."

"Were you . . . did you . . ." Townsend was baffled. Where to begin? What is the proper first question for someone who has seen a whole century pass? "Were you here the first year that the V&T operated?" he said at last.

Canfield chuckled. "Long before that," he replied. "I seen this town when the ore wagons went whooping down through Devil's Gate loaded with ten tons of rock. Dug some of that rock my own self, a thousand feet and more under where you're sitting right now."

Townsend looked down at his feet as if concerned that the porch might give way and drop him all of that thousand feet. "But you weren't born here? I mean, you're even older than Virginia City, right?"

The deep chuckle came again. "I'm most as old as the Comstock Lode itself, or so ever'body round here thinks."

It seemed to Townsend that it was like climbing into a time machine. Not an old newspaper, not an ancient dusty book, but a real, human memory that reached back a hundred years. "Maybe you should just start wherever you like," he said.

"Have a glass of tea," Jim Canfield said, indicating a pitcher and tumbler beside his elbow. "This may take awhile."

Chapter 1

It weren't the best way to begin life, I suppose. My mama was a slave on the MacBride cotton plantation just outside of Memphis. Her name was Ophilia and she was a house slave, which is different from a field slave . . . better than a field hand. She was young and pretty. Mizz MacBride was a good woman, Mama said. Treated all the workers fair and taught the youngins their ABCs and how to cipher some.

Mostly it weren't a bad life, 'til one morning Ophilia was hanging out the washing and she caught the eye of the young master. She was in her eighteenth year and like I say, she was a pretty woman. The young Master MacBride was twenty. He come home from the college down in Memphis and he took a fancy to Ophilia, sweet-talked her and took her to his bed. Such things happened quite a lot back in them days.

She loved him alright, but no good ever come of it. All the long summer he'd take her by the river or meet her in the woods. Then summer come to an end and he went on back to Memphis while Ophilia stayed on the plantation.

Long about November there weren't no hiding the fact that Ophilia's belly was all swelling up and no field hand on the whole plantation would claim the child.

Old man MacBride, he figured out that whenever Ophilia had been off somewheres doing something, the young Mister always found some reason why he ought to leave the house, and that the two of them always come back looking weary and kinda sly. So old man MacBride, he cornered Ophilia and she admitted what went on all summer.

The end of all that was that the old Mister took Ophilia on down to New Orleans and put her on the auction block. She fetched a high price because it was clear that buying her was like buying a mare in foal: two for the price of one.

I was born in New Orleans in February of 1838. There I was, the color of coffee splashed with cream, but still as much a slave as any called nigger in the South. I don't remember nothing about them first years. Mama worked in the kitchen so the two of us was never hungry.

Long about the time I was weaned, the master lost Mama and me in a game of chance played with Colonel Georges, who was famous for fighting with Jackson in the War of 1812. He later made his fortune by running some of the finest bawdy houses in New Orleans.

That's where my first memories begin. He put my mama to work in the kitchen of a place called Madame Nellie's. Mama was a good cook and she had lost her figure by then or it might not have turned out so good for her. The cookhouse was in back of the main building and Mama and I slept in a little lean-to just behind it. I hardly ever went into the main house. It was like some kind of palace to me—all shimmering lights and music drifting out in the nights.

Anyway, I spent my first years turning the spit in the kitchen. Colonel Georges always had fresh cooked beef or a suckling pig over the fire. Only the best food for his customers, he said. I had me a good strong pair of arms at an early age.

Later on, when I was about six, Madame Nellie took a look at me and said how I ought to be dressed up in a turban and silk knickers and pointy Persian slippers. Said I could walk around the parlor with a tray of champagne and serve it to the menfolk who come to relax at the house.

So they decked me in that rig and made out I was a little prince come from some faraway place; India, I think it was. In the daytime I still turned the spit and chopped the kindling, but come evening I carried a silver tray with crystal glasses to the fancy ladies and their old gentlemen callers.

To this day I close my eyes and hear the piany music. I can see them women in their feathers and satin gowns. The reception room was all red silk walls and potted palms and mahogany woodwork.

For all that, life weren't easy for them girls, and girls they was too. I know that now. But they was good to me and Mama. They're long gone, but I can still call them all by name these ninety years later.

I don't remember much about the menfolk who come calling. Their brocade vests were stretched across big bellies hung with gold watch chains and their top hats were a'hanging on the coatrack.

All of us in that house was property of one sort or

another. Colonel Georges owned us all. We was put on this earth to serve the gentlemen who come to Madame Nellie's. Long as we did that, we was alright. Madame Nellie took a strop at me on occasion if I didn't move fast enough, but I seldom got in real trouble, except for one time.

I was forbid to climb the stairs, but once I got curious about what was going on up there in them rooms and I spied through a keyhole and got myself caught. Madame Nellie, who was a big woman, caught me up by my ear and dragged me hollering out to the cookhouse. She told Mama what I was up to and Mama walloped me to an inch of my life. I didn't go up them stairs no more after that.

So it all continued until long about the time I turned ten or so.

Like I said, I was never hungry and I ate a lot too. I begun to sprout up like a weed. Grew out of my silk India suit twice that winter. My arms poked out the sleeves of my jacket from the elbow down. Worse than that, I got real clumsy. I'd stretch out my hand to pick up a glass of whiskey from the piany, misjudge it altogether and knock it off instead.

So I couldn't be a little prince no more. Time come when the men callers started to notice I weren't small no longer and they didn't like it that I was among the ladies carrying drinks. Colonel Georges thought to move my duties entirely out back to the cookhouse again, but Madame Nellie had a gentleman caller named Berger, from Natchez, who said he had a pair of twin niggers about five years old and that I would grow up to make one find drover—strong. He supposed I could be trained to work with the stock in no time.

"I got no use for the two youngins," Berger told the colonel. "Their mama died and they're no good to me on the plantation. I'll make an even swap of them for this young buck of yours," he said.

Colonel Georges puffed his cigar and took a sip of whiskey. He looked at me down on my knees cleaning up something I had just spilled.

Madame Nellie said, "Ophilia won't be happy about it."

"Jim is half-grown," the colonel observed, sipping his whiskey. "Maybe it is not wise for him to remain here. You told me yourself that you caught him peering through a keyhole at Suzette and the Mayor."

"That was a year ago. Jim is still just a child!" Madame Nellie fought hard to keep me on, but it didn't do no good in the end.

The colonel said that Mama would get used to me being gone, because he would put the two little niggers in her care and she would be comforted. And besides, they could wear the silk knickers and turbans I'd growed out of, so it wouldn't cost him a thing. I ate as much as two or three youngins put together and it seemed like a more than fair trade to him.

And so it was that I was sold away from Mama forever. I never did see the two youngins that took my place there at Madame Nellie's bawdy house. Mister Berger sent a fore-man named Ward to fetch me away the day after my eleventh birthday. They made the two youngins wait on the porch whilst I said my farewells. Mama was crying fit to bust.

"My baby boy! My baby! They'll bow your straight back

pickin' cotton. Draggin' a sack! I ain't never gonna see my Jim no more this side of heaven!"

Madame Nellie wiped a tear from her eye and put a hand on Mama's shoulder. "Now then, 'Philia, honey. He's practically grown. You gotta let him go sometime. Mister Berger's a fair man. Said he'd put Jim to apprentice with the drovers." Then she looked at me. "You won't mind, will you, Jim? Learn to drive a team? Workin' with the mules? A man's work for a real man. And maybe one day you'll drive a team right into New Orleans and come to see your mama."

It sounded interesting. I said I would not mind, and truth to tell, anything sounded better than cleaning up cigar ash and serving whiskey to a batch of drunken old men. It had the sound of adventure to me.

Mama said that she supposed it would be better for me to be out in the fresh air than working in a house of temptation after all. "No offense, Madame Nellie," Mama added.

"None taken, 'Philia," Madame Nellie said. "Altogether right. My own child is off to a private school in Charleston. I wouldn't let him near the place, myself."

That was the first time Madame Nellie had ever mentioned she had a child of her own. Just like some slave, that woman had give up her little baby. The thought of that made me sad inside for her. She took my face in her hands and kissed the top of my head. "You're a good boy, Jim," she said. "You'll make a better man than the men I've known." Then Madame Nellie told me to work hard and never to peer through keyholes.

Mama told me not to forget to say my prayers like she had taught. Then she give me a poke full of vittles to feed me on the way, kissed me good-bye, and I left with the foreman, Mister Ward.

———•••———

It didn't matter a pin what Mister Berger promised Colonel Georges about putting me to apprentice with the drovers. I can see that clearly now. Once that foreman tucked my bill of sale into his carpetbag, I didn't belong to the colonel or Madame Nellie or my mama no more.

It was February. We wasn't more than three blocks from home when it started raining the way it always rains in New Orleans in February: hard.

I had me an old blanket to cover my head, but my feet was bare. Ward had himself a black oiled rain slicker he put on over his tan suit. He told me to carry his valise and to walk behind him respectful-like. He said that I should use my blanket to cover up his valise and that it better not get wet.

"You call me Boss, y'heah?" Boss Ward shot me a mean look that made me forget all about the adventure.

"Yessir."

"Yessir what?"

"Yessir, Boss."

"You ain't with your mama no more, boy. Colonel Georges don't own you no more, nor Madame Nellie neither. Don't think you gonna have it so easy as you had livin' with them gals."

"Nawsir, Boss."

"You think you're somethin' better 'cause you're a half-breed mulatter, but to my way of thinkin' a mulatter is one step lower than pure black. You're somethin' I wipe off'n my boots, boy, an' don't you forget it."

I plumb lost my voice after that. He smacked me one across the face and told me to answer when I was spoke to. I said, "Yessir, Boss."

I had me such a feeling of hate inside like I never had before. All this and I weren't no more than ten minutes' walk away from my mama.

Boss Ward was a small, wiry man with sunk-in cheeks on account of he had lost his back teeth. His four front teeth was all yellowed from smoking black cigars. His eyes was small and sharp beneath the shadow of his hat brim. Truth to tell, I thought he looked like the rat I had caught in a bucket when it had been sneaking eggs out in the henhouse some time back. Mama had killed that rat with an ax handle and had said how there weren't much in the world more wicked looking than the face of an egg-sucking rat. I thought about this when I looked at Boss Ward. It made me shiver inside, and not because I was cold, neither. I thought about that ax handle. I had felt sorry for the rat, but I wouldn't feel sorry for Boss Ward if he got hisself caught in a bucket somewheres.

The sky grew darker and the rain poured down heavier than I ever remembered. Maybe I just hadn't noticed how hard the rain could fall before this. Afar off, the lightning forked across the sky and stabbed at the water of the gray delta. Seconds passed and the rumble of thunder rolled over the city and pounded inside me like a big drum. I worried what would happen if Boss Ward's carpetbag got wet. By and by we come to the wharf where a big stern-wheeler was to take us to Natchez the next morning.

The downpour did not slow the work on the docks. Ragged black-skinned men without coats kept on with their work while their white overseers gathered beneath the shed roofs and smoked and talked and warmed their hands over open fires. Great huge crates and barrels and bales come rolling in and out of the warehouses and up and down the gangways of ships and off and onto the freight wagons. Like an ant hill, it was. And those workers that did the lifting and the hauling were of no more consequence than the teams of mules hitched to the freight wagons.

Through the center of all this bustle there come a line of twenty black men chained together hand and foot. They shuffled on past the dockhands whilst two white men with guns pushed and cursed them. The shackled men was loaded onto a stern-wheeler and chained to a post on the open deck.

Of course I had seen such things before. New Orleans was the center of the slave market . . . auctions every day. But I had never thought on it much. What I mean is, I never felt like I was any kind of a slave until just that minute when Boss Ward said what he said about me being a mulatter and so low and all. Folks being bought and sold and taken where they didn't want to go? What did that have to do with me?

Then it come to me all of a sudden that I was one of them. It was like looking into a mirror the first time and seeing that you ain't what you thought you was. The face looking back ain't the same face you expected to see.

I wanted nothing so much as to turn tail and run back to Madame Nellie's bawdy house. Wouldn't do me no good though, I figured. Boss Ward would just find me, take me back and hide me good and brand me with a hot iron like I heard tell was done to runaways.

I was still half-numb at discovering my kinship when Boss Ward gave me a shove toward the tavern called the Three Bales. A painted sign with three cotton bales hung over the door. A plume of wood smoke rose up from the brick chimney and two men dressed in seafaring clothes went in just ahead of us.

The room was dim and hazy but what I noticed first was that it was warm from a great open hearth fireplace that blazed at the back of a room crowded with long tables. The hum of conversation and laughter nearly drowned out Boss Ward's words so he leaned his pointed face down close to me.

His breath was foul. "You wait here with the baggage, mulatter, whilst I have me some refreshment. And don't get no ideas about runnin' off." He popped me hard beneath my chin, then shook his slicker off and tossed it at me. "Hang it up."

I did as I was told, all the while keeping my eyes fixed on that fine blazing fire. I thought about the big fire in the cookhouse at home and how if Mama saw me this wet through and through, she would scold me and strip me and wrap me up and make me drink warm milk in front of the fire. Only one hour separated me from my old life. Poor Mama. If she could see me now, looking like a half-drowned puppy.

Boss Ward bought a pint of rum and sat hisself down at the table nearest to me. I suppose this was so he could be within one long stride of catching me up by my hair should I take to my heels. Three swells sat across from him with their backs to me. Boss supped his rum and talked with the swells, pointing to me and telling them that he had to keep a close watch on me because I was just sold and never been away from my mama before now. He said that once he got me on the boat to Natchez that I wouldn't be no trouble because there weren't no way off except to jump in the river, which was a mile wide.

The three turned around like they was one face and looked my way, then they turned back and begun to talk about what was happening in California in the gold fields. By the time they had drunk three rounds they was all red in the face and loud and excited. People was picking up nuggets by the bucketful just off the ground, they told Boss Ward. And millionaires was being made every day. They had paid their passage to Captain Vickers of the *Flying Witch,* a three-masted schooner set to sail that very night around the Horn to San Francisco. Only fools and cowards were staying behind in the States and missing such an opportunity to strike it rich!

"You're a strong, capable-looking young fellow," said one of the men to Boss. "Why don't you come along?"

Boss said he didn't have money for the fare, or he would join them in a minute. He was twenty-seven and felt like he was wasting his life. He allowed how he was weary of tending niggers and running the plantation of a rich man and having nothing of his own to show for it. He reckoned that his employer owed him a lot more than just wages and that he would never receive what he was truly worth to the plantation.

Now I was sitting there beside the valise, just sort of

drowsing in and out. I would just begin to get warm when someone would open the door to come in or go out and I would be hit again by a blast of cold air. I missed the part of the conversation that was to seal my fate and set me on a course that was altogether different than I imagined.

One minute I was staring at the flames of the fire and the next minute I was lifted up by the scruff and poked and pinched and examined by a half-dozen men in fancy coats.

"Mulatter."

"Quadroon or half?"

"Half." Boss had the look of a man who had made up his mind about something. "I've got the bill of sale. It says he's half. Good combination. Smarts of a white man and the strength of a . . ."

"Mulatters sometimes get high-minded. Uppity," argued a man with a heavy gold watch chain draped across a dark red silk vest.

"He does as he's told," Boss Ward snapped, "don't you, boy?"

"Yessir, Boss," I said.

The big-bellied man leaned closer to me like he was going to sniff my head. "Wait a minute . . . ain't this the child from . . . don't I know you, boy?"

I had seen plenty of swoll-gutted gentlemen around Madame Nellie's, but I never looked at their faces much. "I don't know, mister."

"Ain't you the child from down at Nellie's? All dressed up in the turban and the Persian slippers? Carry the tray around?"

"Yessir, I is," I told him.

"Well, then." The big-bellied man seemed pleased. "I know this child." He turned to Boss. "Colonel Georges let him go to you?"

"A trade." Boss Ward fumbled for the bill of sale, which said plain as anything that one male slave aged eleven years had been traded for two five-year-old male children and that Frank Ward had taken possession thereof. "Now all I want is enough cash in hand to buy my fare to San Francisco and one hundred dollars besides. You can put this boy on the auction block in the morning and make a clear one hundred dollar profit on the deal."

I looked up at the face of the big-paunched man. He tugged his moustache and scratched behind his ear while he thought the proposition over. I was hoping he would go for it. Anything would be better than spending the rest of my life under the fist of Boss Ward.

Big Belly sucked his teeth awhile and squeezed my arm like I was a hog on the hoof. Then he reached into his pocket and took out his money belt. He made me stand and warm myself by the fire lest I catch the pneumonia and die before he could sell me. The papers was drawn transferring ownership to him. This was signed by witnesses, including a judge who also recognized me from Nellie's and said I ought to fetch a good price.

So it was that Boss Ward sailed away to the gold fields and I was put on the auction block after only one night away from my mama.

Chapter 2

Next morning the auctioneer asked the fella what bought me from Boss Ward what kind of experience I had. The auctioneer thought he said I was well mannered and hard working and had spent my entire life working around the "horses" at the house that belonged to a certain famous colonel of the War of 1812.

Of course four-legged critters ain't what was meant. All the same, as I stood on the block I was passed off as a first-rate stable hand to that crowd. Yessir! By the time that auctioneer got finished calling off my bona fides I was most convinced myself that I could handle a team and hitch any harness to a rig in less time than it took to say, "Whoa!"

Because of this misunderstanding, I fetched a high price, and also because my teeth was good and I was big for my age, which meant I was sure to grow bigger and stronger and there was a whole lot of life in me and long years of service.

The hammer come down hard on the table.

"Sold! To Mister Hezikiah Green, of Green Freight and Livery, Flora, Missouri, for four hundred thirty-seven dollars!"

Young Hezikiah Green counted out the money in gold coin and the papers was signed. He looked me over real good as we loaded up to get on that riverboat.

"Ain't I seen you someplace, boy?"

I looked him over real good too. He was a tall, strong, youngish sort of man. He had dark side whiskers and a tall beaver hat, which made him even taller. He wore a long black and tan checkered coat with matching trousers. His jaw was big and he had the sort of face that the girls at Nellie's would have called handsome, I reckon. He had a happy, befuddled sort of way about him—like a proud hound dog trotting home with a varmint to lay on the porch. His eyes was bright blue but bloodshot, and he smelled of the drink. Other than that I could not see that he had any disgusting habits.

"I don't rightly know if you seen me," I answered truthful.

"It'll come to me." He scratched his head under his hat and shielded his eyes against the sun, which had just busted out and made a rainbow over the river like some kind of a sign. "My lucky day." He rubbed his hands together.

I decided to take my chances and keep my mouth shut that I had never been around horses. I was afraid he'd take me back to the auctioneer and turn me in for his money and I wouldn't get to learn to drive a team after all.

It was getting on toward noon when the lines was cast off and that big old paddlewheel boat took to churning up the muddy Mississippi. I still had most of a whole fried chicken in my poke that Mama had sent me off with. Hezikiah Green stood at the rail as New Orleans slid away and I sat down on a crate. I offered him a piece of chicken and a corn dodger and he took it and was right congenial about how good it were and how it was seldom that a man could find chicken cooked this good.

"My mama fix it for me," I told him.

"This your first time away from your mama?" He chewed the last bit of chicken off the drumstick and flung the bone away into the foaming water behind the wheel.

"Yessir. My mama is the cook at Madame Nellie's bawdy house. Some say she is the finest cook this side of . . ." It just slipped out.

Green got a real peculiar look on his face. "I know your mama's chicken, boy," he said. "And I know Madame Nellie too." He crossed his arms and stuck out his lower lip.

"Mebbe that where you seen me before."

He got real quiet. I gave him another good piece of fried chicken and he ate it slow, then wiped the grease off his chin with a kerchief. "You growed up some. Growed right out of that silk turban and them Persian slippers since last time I come to New Orleans. I was there at Nellie's last night, and there was these two little scrawny youngins wearin' your outfits. I heard you got traded off."

The thought of it made me real sad. "Yessir. I growed too big and they got shed of me. Now I'll never taste my mama's fried chicken no more, I reckon."

"But you ain't never been a stable hand." He said this with a sideways look to his face.

"Nawsir, I ain't."

"Uncle Trueblood ain't gonna like this much. Told me to get on down to New Orleans and pick us up a groom. Now what?" He looked miserable.

"Mama says I learn real quick. I know my ABCs and how to cipher."

He didn't say no more to me for most the rest of the day. Night settled in cloudy, black, and starless. Inside the bright parlor of that riverboat they was playing banjo and piany just like back home. Hezikiah Green was inside, but I wasn't allowed. I waited where I was told. I listened to that music and the rushing slap, slap, slap of the paddle on the water and I must have dozed a bit. After awhile he come out and went into a sleeping cabin on the upper deck. I could smell he had been drinking and I settled down on a blanket outside his door.

I was mighty lonesome away from Mama, so I finished off the rest of my grub. Except I saved out one last corn dodger which eventually petrified so I could carry it for a lucky piece like a yeller chunk of rock.

When the morning come I woke up inside the cabin of Hezikiah Green. Sometime in the night he had moved me in to bunk on the floor beside the steam pipes where it weren't so cold. It was good of him. I have always thought so.

I woke up hungry as Daniel's lions in the den. Hezikiah was already up and dressed and pulling on his boots when I come round.

"Well it only figures you'd be a late sleeper comin' from where you come from." He nudged me with the toe of his boot, then took hold of the blanket and gave it a jerk, spilling me out. "It ain't gonna do when Uncle Trueblood gets hold of you. You'll be up before the sun and no breakfast 'til you've finished feedin' the stock."

I sat up and looked at my empty poke. I wished I hadn't

eat all my grub. "How long 'til we get where we goin'?" I was thinking about food.

"A few days."

"I'll be dead by then, if I don't eat."

"You got chores to do boy, before you taste anything but sawdust in your mouth."

He jerked me up and threw me out of the cabin. It was bitter cold. The day was slate gray and everything in the world seemed to blend into the wide river. He gave me the boot forward to where a wood crate was marked in black letters GREEN FRT. CO.

"What's that say, boy?" He pointed at the letters.

I got the part that spelled *Green,* but botched the rest and he give me another kick.

"Green Freight Company! And don't you forget it!" he hollered. "And inside that box is your road to breakfast. I got me four fine, filthy, used saddles in there. Bought at auction where folks know the difference 'tween a horse and a bawdy house!" He pried up the lid. "Now, boy, here's saddle soap and a brush and a rag. I'm gonna show you how to clean a saddle proper and then you're gonna do it before you get your mouth around one spoonful of grits. You gonna know how it's done before you meet Uncle Trueblood, or I'm gonna pitch you in that river one piece at a time and use you for catfish bait."

There was other people on that boat, but they didn't pay his hollering no mind. I was his and they didn't butt in. It was clear to everyone that this man had hisself a no-good, and that I needed to be taught a lesson.

I was sorry I shared Mama's chicken with him.

Before noon I learned how to soap a saddle proper—
four of them. I finally ate me a piece of bread with two
slices of bacon and then Hezikiah Green started me on the
harness, which I finished too late for supper. After that I
didn't think so kindly of him no more, but I reckon he was
just trying to save his own skin from the shock of when his
Uncle Trueblood met me and found out I didn't know nothing about what I was bought for.

By the time we reached Missouri I had cleaned every
piece of tack six or seven times and knew the name of
everything from cinch to singletree. I count myself lucky
that there weren't no horses nor wagons on that riverboat
or he would have had me driving a six-up team full gallop
around the deck.

※

Young Hezikiah Green's uncle was named Elwood
Langford Rupert Trueblood Green. It was a mighty long
name for such a little, sawed-off old man. He had a streak
of mean and ornery that matched the length of his name.

To his face, most folks called him Mister Trueblood
Green. Behind his back they called him Bloodhound, Bloodsucker, or old Blood-and-Guts, depending on which one of
his businesses they was involved with. And once he got it
in his mind he wanted something, most everyone just called
him Uncle and give in to him.

Old Trueblood owned near half of everything in that
little town. Not that Flora, Missouri, was much to own. It
was a little collection of white clapboard buildings all snuggled together behind the levy. There was the Rupert House
hotel and Flora's Restaurant just beside the Elwood Cotton

Gin and Warehouse. Folks drew their meager earnings at the Langford Bank and spent them at the Trueblood Mercantile and Drygoods. Then there was Green Freight and Livery.

That took up every family name of the old skinflint. The only one I didn't connect right off was Flora's Restaurant. Young Hezikiah explained that Flora was old Trueblood's mama. She was long passed on, but Trueblood memorialized her cooking in that eating house with the most pitiful-tasting food cooked from her own recipes. A man had to be half starved or a stranger or in debt to Trueblood to eat a meal at Flora's.

The town was also named after Trueblood's mama.

There was three churches for the white folks who lived in and around Flora.

The Methodist Church was attended by Republicans and that minority of the town that weren't owned by Trueblood. The Catholic church was downright deserted except for the priest and a handful of old coots and widows from the days when there was a French outpost along the river. The most crowded church in Flora was the Free Will Baptist, which was different from Southern Baptist and Primitive Baptist.

The Free Will Baptist Church of Flora, Missouri, was chockful of Democrats and was attended by everyone who worked for old man Trueblood or owed him a penny.

The old man would foreclose the mortgage and repossess the property of a Republican Methodist without blinking an eye. On the other hand, he'd give special dispensation to debtors who were Democrats, provided they were also regularly attending members of the Free Will Baptist congregation.

And then there was what old Trueblood called "the darkie church, set up for those hapless sons of the mark of Cain, where no white man dast put his foot."

This was the one place in Flora where those of us that was slaves could congregate peacefully on the Sabbath Day. We could sing and glory and study how the Lord freed the Hebrew slaves and contemplate sedition according to the Good Book.

But I am getting ahead of my story.

On the day I stepped off that Mississippi riverboat onto the levy of Flora, I didn't know none of this.

All I knowed was that Hezikiah run the livery and freight office for his Uncle Trueblood. Hezikiah had bought me for his Uncle Trueblood's business. Hezikiah had drummed terror into my head about Mister Trueblood and I landed expecting to see a Goliath of a man with a long black bullwhip who would beat me if I didn't know the difference between a hame and a halter. Hezikiah told me to stay behind him until he had a chance to tell his uncle that I weren't fully growed. His Uncle Trueblood would be expecting someone bigger than me, Hezikiah supposed, and he wanted to explain what a bargain I had been.

I was looking all around for someone big and mean-looking, but all I seen was a bent old fella with a cane that come shuffling toward me and Hezikiah. A toothless old man he was, with a black suit dusted with dandruff and a high collar that cut into the flesh of his sagging jowls. His elbows was turned out and his knees was bent like he had tried to sit down and got stuck halfway.

He waved his cane. "So nephew!" he hollered real pleasant like. "Where's the new man?"

Hezikiah gulped and blinked and sweat popped out on his brow even though it were cold. "I got fine saddles and English-made harness at the . . ."

"Where's the new man?" Trueblood's toothless mouth screwed around in a squawk. "Old Dimmy's gonna die one of these days and I ain't gonna leave that room at the stable empty, I told ye! Now, where's my new slave ye brung?"

"I got a good'n, Uncle Trueblood. He'll work out real good."

Trueblood was squinting his eyes up at the deck of the boat where a big, strong, ebony-colored man was hauling down the crates marked GREEN FRT. CO.

"How much did he cost, Hezikiah? That's a nine-hundred-dollar slave if he's a penny! I tole ye stay in the budget I give ye!"

"And I did, Uncle! Four hundred fifty! And he's . . ."

"What is he? A countraband? Is he stole from somebody else? I tole ye I wouldn't have no countraband propity! If ye got that man for four hundred and fifty . . ." He shook his cane in the face of the big slave, who scowled at him and dumped a crate at his feet, then turned back to the boat.

"It ain't him," Hezikiah muttered and stepped aside. He reached back and grabbed me by the scruff of my shirt. "This is him. He's smart as a whip and strong. Young enough so as to be trained proper."

Trueblood turned white, then red, then purple as he sized me up. Hezikiah repeated the yarn the auctioneer had told about how I spent my whole life around horses and worked for a famous colonel who fought with Andy Jackson in 1812. He explained what a willing lad I was and that I could do nothing but become a credit to the business.

Trueblood whacked me on the arm with his cane. "Ye paid that for this?" he shrieked at poor Hezikiah. "Ye're tellin' me that this is gonna replace old Dimmy when he's gone over yonder?"

"Now, now, Uncle Trueblood! One day, if I handle it right and do right by it, and manage the business in a prudent manner, you have promised that Green Freight and Livery would be . . ."

"I'll see lawyer Cousin Langford about yer part in my will and change it tomorrow!"

"I like this boy! He's bright, I say! Ask him anything you want about how to harness . . ."

"Ye are a fool, Hezikiah Green! Paid twice as much as ye should for a mulatter child who anybody can see has soft hands! Look at them blisters!" He grabbed up my hands and then flung me back. I fell on the levy, then jumped up and went around out of the old man's reach behind the crate of saddles. I noticed folks was looking with pity at poor Hezikiah.

"He'll work out," Hezikiah pleaded. "Dimmy will teach him, and look at the long years of service we're sure to get out of him!"

"And I'll be long gone by then! What profit is there for me in that? A bad bargain!"

"He'll learn quick."

"He'd better! Yessir! Or I will see about my will!"

As old Trueblood shuffled away, folks on either side tipped their hats and greeted him like he were the king or something. But he paid them no mind. Just muttered and grumbled on down the boardwalk. Then I seen everybody wagging their heads and looking over at Hezikiah Green and at me.

I do believe that Hezikiah would have sold me right then and there at a loss if anybody had been willing, but it was plain to see that owning me would be a liability in a town like Flora. The old bloodsucker was sure to curse and spit every time he cast his dim eye my way.

Hezikiah turned round, give me a hard look, then jerked his head toward the street, which led right to Green Freight and Livery. "Let's go see what Uncle Dimmy can do with you."

And so it was that I come under the watchful care of old Uncle Dimmy.

Now Uncle Dimmy was probably older than Uncle Trueblood, but he was just the exact opposite in nature.

Hezikiah called Trueblood "Uncle" because of blood kinship and that legal tie-in with the old skinflint's last will and testament. It was more a political decision than one of affection.

Uncle Dimmy, however, was called "Uncle" because everybody liked to consider him some sort of a family member, even though he was black as a beetle and ancient as Methuselah. Uncle Dimmy always said that after a man gets older than everybody else, white folks don't remember no more what color he is or where he come from, they just sort of admire the fact that he lived so long. They come by and say howdy in hopes that some of that long life and luck will rub off on them.

Well, when I first seen Uncle Dimmy, I reckon I didn't think about being an old man myself someday. Mister Hezikiah told me as we walked toward the barn that Uncle Dimmy had been a boy my age in Virginia when the Declaration of Independence was writ. That didn't mean much to me in them days. It had nothing to do with my freedom, did it? And he was still a slave, weren't he?

He was real old. I guess that's what I'm trying to make clear. Even so, he was in better shape than Trueblood, who owned him, just like he owned the horses and mules at Green Freight and Livery.

"Now listen to me, boy," Hezikiah warned. "I'm turning you over to Uncle Dimmy and you'll do everything he tells you, hear?"

"Yessir."

"He'll make you fit enough to suit Uncle Trueblood Green."

In the yard, all the wagons and buggies was parked in a large covered shed. Three shaggy horses milled around in a corral beside the barn. One of the animals give another a kick, laid back his ears, and chased him off the feed as they will do. Truth to tell, I hadn't been much around horses and they looked mighty big and intimidating to me. I missed my mama.

The barn doors was wide open and it was dark inside. We stood there a minute and I couldn't see nothing. But I heard the stirring of the animals in their stalls, a soft nicker. I smelled the sweet smell of horses and hay. A warm, friendly scent it was; I love the smell of a barn to this day. Then the sun come out and shined down on the barn roof. Shafts of light beamed down through some missing shingles. Specks of dust swirled around in the air and I could see the hayloft above long rows of stalls and the fine strong heads of the horses looking out at us as we come in. There was a small office with a desk just to the right of the door and a potbellied stove. To the left was a long, low-ceilinged tack room dripping with harnesses and horse collars and lined with rows of fine saddles sitting on barrels.

"Uncle Dimmy!" Mister Hezikiah hollered real loud. "I brung you a new colt to break!"

There was more stirring in the stalls. A black-and-white cat come out carrying a mouse in its jaws. It run over toward a door beneath the shadow of the hayloft and there I seen my first look at Uncle Dimmy. His face was so black I couldn't make it out in the shadow, but his hair was white as the stripe on that cat's nose. He was tall and lean and only bent a little at the shoulders—in good shape for a fella as old as the United States of America.

"Well now, Pickle," he said to the cat, "I thought you said you brung me a colt to break. Dis ain't nuthin' but a leetle ol' mouse." Then he laughed and picked up the cat and rubbed its ears while the mouse still dangled there.

Hezikiah give me a little shove forwards into a patch of light. "It's me, Uncle Dimmy, and this is what I brung you."

The old man took a step towards me. I felt like a rabbit must feel when a lantern gets shined in his eyes in the night. I didn't move a step, but I tried to see the old man's face.

"You back, Hezikiah?" he asked. "And you brung me a colt?"

"This boy. This here child is what I mean."

"I thought t'was Pickle talkin' to me." He laughed again and it was a pleasant kind of laugh. "Well now. Well, well, well. Lawd, lawd, lawd! Will you just look at dis!"

He come on toward me stopping just out of the beam's circle where I stood.

"Do he have a name?"

Hezikiah said, "Tell Uncle Dimmy your name, boy."

I answered that my name was Jim.

"Dat'll do." His ancient gnarled grip reached out and took my right hand to hold it palm up. "You ain't did much real work a'fore now, eh Jim?"

Hezikiah answered for me. "He ain't never been away from his mama before this. He come out of the kitchen of a bawdy house in New Orleans and I got him by mistake. But here he is and you have to do somethin' with him, Uncle Dimmy, or Trueblood is gonna have my neck. I worked on teachin' him all the harness parts and cleanin' the saddles fifty times. He's smart enough, but he's a complainer. Must be 'cause he come from a kitchen an' his mama let him eat whenever he want to. Got an appetite like a half-starved goat."

Uncle Dimmy stepped into the light. His eyes was smiling and his face was all lines like the rivers and roads on a map. The whites of his eyes was pale yellow, same as paper turned with age. He didn't have no teeth, but he grinned with his gums.

"You'll do, chile," he said, and he patted me on the shoulder kind of like I was a quivering colt about to bolt on out the corral gate. "Easy now, chile. You do as Uncle Dimmy say an' we's gwine t'git on fine."

I said I would, and that was that. He pointed up the ladder to the hayloft, then told me all the straw in the stalls needed turning and the manure shoveled. There was a wheelbarrow, and a shovel and a pitchfork hung right there on the wall; he said everything had a place and he expected that I ought to learn that place and put it all right where it needed to be when I was finished.

All of this made Hezikiah shake his head with relief. "He'll work out, won't he Uncle Dimmy?"

"He will."

"I knew you could take him in hand."

I was ready to get to work, but Uncle Dimmy set the timetable in that barn.

"I gots me a skillet o' catfish t'fry up fust." He put his boney arm round my shoulder, then said to Hezikiah, "You get on home, Hez. An' don' worry y'self none. Me an' young Jim gonna have us a bite t'eat, then we's gwine t'git dis barn clean up 'fore bedtime."

—•◦•◦•—

First evening, after the stalls was all clean and the critters fed, old Uncle Dimmy popped us corn and drizzled butter on it. He didn't salt it none because my hands was all sore and blistered.

We sat up awhile by the lantern light and he had me tell him the very first thing I remembered about my life. So I told him about my mama and the way the kitchen smelled when she was making plum jelly . . . how the kettle boiled a deep red and how she skimmed the sugar foam off with a wood ladle and give it to me to lick. Whilst I tasted that sweetness she told me stories from the Good Book and sung me hymns and such. That was the first thing I remembered. It made my mouth water for that sugared ladle, and her voice come to mind clear as anything.

Uncle Dimmy said what a good woman my mama was. Then he done the same for me; telling me the first thing he remembered about his mama and what she looked like eighty some years before when she was taking the laundry off the line and how the sheets was stiff and how they smelled like sweet peas because they had dried by the garden.

It was something, hearing that old man talk on like that. I could almost smell the flowers and hear his mama talk to me, even though them sweet peas had bloomed eighty summers before!

He finished talking and I didn't feel so lonesome no more. I was most tired I had ever been by then. Popcorn all ate up, he told me to go wash myself in the trough and brush my teeth with a twig. Then he slathered my blisters with bag balm, which is medicine for the sore udders of milk cows and such, but it works for blisters on humans too. He stuck my hands into a pair of clean socks like to bandage them.

"Does you know how t'say yo' prayers?" he asked me.

I told him that my mama taught me.

"Sweet Jesus jus' as sweet to a man's soul as lickin' dat plum jelly ladle." He got down on his old knees and prayed like his mama taught him, and I got down on my young knees and said my prayers like my mama told me to and I was satisfied body and soul.

Chapter 3

So my life in Flora with Uncle Dimmy moved along day by day in the same way, winter, spring, summer, and fall, for six years. I growed into my big feet there at Green Freight and Livery Company. Uncle Dimmy fed me, taught me everything he knowed about horses and mules, and treated me as kindly as if I was his own child. We spent them years swapping stories until I knowed his all by heart. I have written all of Uncle Dimmy's life down in a separate book, and it is almost as thick as my own. But that is for another time.

February, 1856, come round and I turned eighteen years old. I was near to six feet four inches tall, and Uncle Dimmy said someday I was going to be stout as an oak, though I was still skinny as a birch tree. He told old Trueblood that young Hezikiah had got a bargain in me and that if Trueblood left the business to anyone else but Hez, that Uncle Dimmy might take it into his mind to be a runaway and take me north with him!

Business was mighty slow and Trueblood blamed Hez for its failing. Trueblood didn't pay Uncle Dimmy no mind. He said Uncle Dimmy was too old to run anywheres and that Hezikiah was a fool and that Trueblood didn't plan on dying anytime soon.

As I got taller, it seem to me that Uncle Dimmy just got more shrunk up. He was a little more bent, a little more hard of hearing, and his head shook from side to side like he was always saying no.

"Uncle Dimmy? You want a pan of corn bread?" I asked him.

His head wobbled, "No."

Then he would say, "Shore would be good to have me some corn bread."

I had to ignore his head.

His hands shook so that I had to do all the cooking and such. It had been a long time since he tended the mules. I made him a willow rocking chair that Christmas and he just set beside the potbellied stove and rocked and told stories and dozed.

White folks would come by and ask him if he was feeling well. His old head said no, but he would smile and say he was going home to see his mama and Jesus by and by. He would ask them white folks if they would like to have a last supper with him before he went.

Last suppers was usually whatever I had cooked up at the time. Now I was a fine cook. From all them years I had spent in my mama's kitchen and then with old Dimmy making me repeat every recipe I could remember, cooking come to me real natural.

Folks started dropping in of a morning to speak to Uncle Dimmy because they was certain he would invite them to have a last supper of my coffee, biscuits, and gravy. And then passengers off the riverboats would stop in for the noon meal because I had recollected the way my mama used to make fried chicken and I could make it most as good as she had.

About this time a light come on in Uncle Dimmy's brain. He seen that folks in Flora and the people who got off the riverboats to get a bite to eat while the boats took on cargo was positively in revolt about the slop served at Flora's Restaurant. Biscuits there was hard as meadow muffins baked in the sun. It was said that the chicken and dumplings served at Flora's could cause blindness because a fella could go blind looking for the chicken. So, it come to Uncle Dimmy that folks who dropped in for a last supper maybe ought to pay something.

He set up a sign on an empty coffee tin:

UNCLE DIMMY'S BURIAL FUND

Under the sign was a list of prices for biscuits, fried chicken, jars of jelly, and the like.

It started out real small, but Uncle Dimmy emptied out the can every day and sent me down to buy supplies. Hezikiah caught the vision and hired a freeman to help with the barn so I could cook all day. He moved the tack and set up some tables and benches in the tack room. Hezikiah's wife, Nancy, made gingham curtains and tablecloths and napkins and such and they brung their big cookstove down for me to cook on.

It was a wonder and a miracle. The hoot of the big paddle wheeler whistle would sound, and I would get to frying because we knowed for certain that folks was going to swarm in like hogs to the trough!

Uncle Dimmy just sat in that willow rocking chair beside the potbellied stove and greeted folks as they come in. His can for the burial fund was still there, only now the sign for meal prices was posted big and plain above the counter. Uncle Dimmy would rattle his can and say howdy once again after the folks had already paid Miss Nancy for their meals. They all felt obliged to drop something in the old man's offering so as he might buy a fancy casket for his Great Gettin' Up Mornin'!

In this way Hezikiah Green got himself a real business. It was a going concern, I will say!

Another sign was painted and hung beneath the freight and livery sign. Big red letters spelled out:

UNCLE DIMMY'S TACK ROOM

Customers got to be real regular. On a certain day of the week we could just about tell who was going to show up according to the schedule of the riverboats. Pilots and deck hands alike marked Uncle Dimmy's Tack Room on their navigation charts. One such customer was a young apprentice pilot, name of Sam, who showed up every Tuesday around noon. Whilst the others took their meals out in the tack room, Sam come back to sit beside the cookstove. That way he'd get a little extra and get to lick the chocolate cake icing from the bowl. I didn't mind him none. He would talk about the old Mississippi and how she wandered all the way from St. Paul to New Orleans, and what he seen on his travels. This put a hankering in me to get on that paddle wheeler one day and leave Flora behind forever. Maybe I could travel north where a man could not be bought nor sold because of his color. I didn't tell nobody what I was thinking.

In them days there was whispers about the Underground Railroad taking slaves to freedom. Sometimes on Sabbath Day the preacher would talk about men in bondage and how they was delivered by the Lord to freedom. Sometimes their slavery was of a physical nature and sometimes it was the slavery of their hearts. Either way the Lord Almighty was in the business of setting captives free and I was a captive. Just like that sweet sugar ladle, them stories from the Good Book and the tales that Sam told me made my soul hungry for freedom of both sorts.

Uncle Dimmy saw this in my eye and he said to me, "Don't nobody get free 'less dey prays fo' an answer. Tell it to Jesus, boy."

So I begun to pray for a plan and a way to get free from old Trueblood. I begun to ask every day that the sea would open and I could march on through.

But I didn't get the kind of answer I expected. When I first seen it, it didn't look anything like a yes. It looked like a no. Worse than no . . .

This is what happened.

In all them years, I still hadn't got back to New Orleans to see my mama and I took to thinking how fine it would be to just show up in her kitchen all growed up and surprise her. I told this to Sam one day whilst he was licking the icing off the bowl.

"Well, why don't you just go on down there then?" He was smiling like he knowed some secret. "You can leave with us. We're headed down to Orleans."

"You know I cain't do such a thing," I told him. "I

belong to old Mister Trueblood. He'd send the bounty man after me if'n I was to leave with y'all."

Sam leaned way back in his chair and sucked the chocolate off that wooden ladle. "Your mama has all those recipes, doesn't she? All the ones you talk about but can't cook?"

"I reckon she do."

"Mister Hezikiah is sure to let you go down and speak to her. You wouldn't be gone more than six days. When you come back you'll have all the secrets to your mama's cooking and there's no telling what that'll do for business here at the Tack Room."

I knowed Sam good enough to know that he didn't do something without expecting something in return.

"What you want for carrying me all that way and back? I got no money for passage."

He twirled that spoon in his fingers and studied on it awhile. "Cook for me every day of your passage. I want chocolate cake and apple fritters and some of that . . ."

He listed every kind of dish I knowed how to cook, and then when his mouth was watering he said he would go speak to Hezikiah on the matter straight away. He jumped up and went to fetch Hezikiah.

Hez and Mizz Nancy thought it might be a real good idea for me to get on down to New Orleans and get all them secret recipes that my mama wouldn't give to nobody else. They told Sam that they would be right pleasured to accept his proposal, but that Mister Trueblood Green had to be consulted on the matter. They said that they would give their answer next Tuesday when the *Mary Belle* stopped at the Flora levy to pick up fuel.

I took to praying real hard that Mister Trueblood Green

would see what a fine idea it was for me to travel on back to New Orleans.

But it was not to be. Same evening, Mister Trueblood hobbled into the barn and started hollering for Hez and Mizz Nancy to get on out of the kitchen and come have a word with him where they belonged . . . in the muck of a stall.

I knowed this was real trouble, so I snuck up into the hayloft and watched the sweet world unravel beneath me.

Trueblood was one mean old man, I can tell you that. He brung along two strong young fellas who sharecropped his land and went to his church. They didn't look none too happy to be there, but they stood just behind Trueblood to add some muscle to his threats. He begun to tell Hez and Mizz Nancy that Uncle Dimmy's Tack Room had took all the eating business away from Flora's Restaurant. He said that the Tack Room was closed forthwith and that I was to go right back to my duties as a stable boy. He said if ever he caught me cooking in Flora again that he would sell me down the river. All the folks at his Baptist church had been told that they was not to come round here no more unless it was to rent a horse and buggy. He told Hez and Mizz Nancy that they was out of the will altogether and that they should pack theirselfs up and leave Flora.

Then Trueblood snapped his fingers, and the two big shamefaced sharecroppers commenced to taking that little dining room apart. They broke the tables and the benches, throwed Mizz Nancy's tablecloths on the floor, ripped down the curtains, and broke the crockery.

Uncle Dimmy sat there in his wicker rocker and he cried like a baby. Mizz Nancy run out of the place and poor Hez cursed that old demon Trueblood and called him what he was. But it didn't make no difference to Trueblood. He owned the place, and he owned me and Uncle Dimmy, and he could do what he wanted.

He hollered at me to come out from where I was. I was scared he would sell me down the river right then, but when he took to shouting at old Uncle Dimmy I come down.

Trueblood whipped me with his cane. It didn't hurt none because I was big and he was an old evil man who had no strength left but his meanness.

"Clean this up, you sneakin', lazy nigger!" he screamed. "If it ain't clean and the saddles and tack all back in place 'fore mornin', you're gone, boy! I'll sell you for a field hand! Then we'll see how proud you are, doin' stoop work in the cotton fields!"

Thus ended my hopes. Our hopes. Everything was broke to pieces. I carried Uncle Dimmy into his bed and commenced to get to work on the tack room. I worked most of the night. I was real mad. It crossed my mind to go on over to Trueblood's house and climb through a window and put a pillow over his head. No one would be sorry. But I didn't do it. I just cleaned up them broken dreams and looked out the window as the sky got pale and perfect the way it does before dawn. And I begun to pray again because I was right scared I might do murder if I didn't find me an answer real soon.

After everything was put back the way it had been, I went in and sat beside Uncle Dimmy's bed. He was sleeping that deep sleep that old men often sleep. Maybe he was dreaming about when he was young because there was a smile on his face. Then of a sudden he opened his eyes.

"What you doin' up s'early, Jim?" He asked me. Then he remembered. His face got cloudy. "You finish?"

"Got it all back the way Bloodsucker say to."

I told him what I had been thinking about doing murder to Trueblood and going to see Mama, and then I confessed I had been thinking a lot about my freedom too.

"Dat's right," he said to me from his pillow. "Light de lamp, child. I done bin thinkin' 'bout crossin' dat river m'self real soon. Bin thinkin' 'bout goin' t'see my mama too."

"Don't talk 'bout dyin', Uncle Dimmy." I patted his hand, which was looking more like the claw of a bird lately. Thinner and thinner he was getting. "When you talk like that it scares me. What am I gonna do round here if you ain't here t'look after me?"

The old man smiled up at me and waved his hand at the pine chest where he kept his things. "Plump up m' pillers an' hep me set up." I did that. Then he said, "Open de chest up, Little Jim," he tells me. "Get out my Great Gittin' Up Mornin' box dere 'neath my long handles."

So I done it.

Now Uncle Dimmy's chest was a cigar box where he hid all his savings from his burial fund. It had a picture of a red Indian on the outside and he kept it closed by a little nail on the top. I knowed it was there all along because he had told me when his Great Gettin' Up Mornin' come that I was supposed to pay the undertaker, Dick Willis, with the money in that box.

So I give the box to Uncle Dimmy. He pried it open and let loose with a kind of cackle, then he slammed the top shut again. He cradled the cigar box like it was a child.

"Gonna go out in style!" he said. "I done had a word wif Undertaker Willis jus' las' week. Done ordered me up a cherrywood coffin wif nickle-plate handles. Gots me a hearse wif six horses wearin' black plumes. You be settin' up on dat carriage wearin' a top hat an' biled shirt. Brass band gonna play me 'Death's Harvest Time' real slow and march behin' whilst we rollin' out t' de graveyard an' all de wimmin gonna cry and moan whilst I is laid low in de grave."

The image pleasured him, but it gave me worse miseries.

"Uncle Dimmy, it ain't time to talk of such things. Please . . ."

"Oh yes it is!" He put up a hand to silence me. "Now I s'pose I is gonna be watchin' all dis like the Good Book say from among dat cloud of witnesses!"

"You got a long time still."

"No, boy, it ain't so."

I was feeling like I was gonna bust with grief, although it ain't even happened yet. But Uncle Dimmy always did tell a good story and paint a tale good enough so as a fella's mind just saw it clear as anything.

"It'll be a mighty fine goin' home," I said to him. "And never mind yourself none. I'll be sure it's all like you want. I'll take your Great Gettin' Up Mornin' money and pay the undertaker just like you want."

Now he busted out laughing. "No, boy! Dat's what I'm a'tellin' you. I done paid Willis fo' ever'thang!" He pried open the box again and waved a receipt from Willis Undertaker's Parlor marked "Paid in Full." And there was everything just like uncle Dimmy told me: casket, hearse, horses, plumes, top hat, and brass band. And at the bottom of the list was a solid granite headstone set to be inscribed with these words:

R.I.P.
DIMMY CANFIELD
b. 1764 d. 1856
BELOVED FATHER OF
JIM CANFIELD

"I didn't know you had a youngin," I said.

"Yessir. I does." He was looking at me, wanting me to catch his meaning, but I did not. "You is my youngin, Jim. Dere it is set in stone. It gives you my name."

Now when I understood this sentiment, I commenced to cry. I laid my weary head in that old man's lap and I bawled like to bust. I never had a father before. And now he give me a name.

He let me bawl awhile, and then he patted me on the shoulder and told me to set up and listen up because he had more to tell me.

He shoved that cigar box into my hands and told me to open it. Which I did.

Inside there was ten double eagle gold pieces staring me in the face. A double eagle was worth twenty dollars in them days. So Uncle Dimmy had two hundred dollars left over from his burial fund! And everything was already paid in full.

He begun to laugh at the look on my face. "Dat hide o' yourn is worth 'bout nine hunert dolluhs, Jim," he said to me. "Now I had hopes t'buy yo' freedom, but it ain't gonna happen. I knows it. Dere ain't enuff time, chile. But I see yo' frien'. I bin watchin' young Sam, de riverboat pilot. He's took a shine t'you."

"Yessir. He likes my cake all right."

"It's enuff. He don' cotton t' Mister Trueblood."

"Nobody do."

"Dat's a fact. But Sam'll hep you when de time come. Dem double eagles b'longs t' you, Jim. I mean fer you t'have dem fer a legacy, chile. As any good pappy ought, I bin savin' fo' my chile. Hide 'em now, an' set tight. When de time come an' I be gone over yonder, fetch up dat treasure an' pay dat riverboat man one double eagle t'carry you north."

* * *

After all that talk 'bout death I was powerful weary. I had not slept for near twenty-four hours, but all the same I cleaned the ashes out of the stove and went to fix biscuits and gravy for Uncle Dimmy's breakfast just like he liked it.

He called to me from his bed, "Little Jim, sing me 'Roll Jordan Roll.'"

So I sung "Roll Jordan," which was his favorite song because he figured the Jordan River must be something like the Mississippi and he loved the wide, slow waters of that river. Whilst I was cooking he called out, "Dat smell real good, don't it?" Then, "Dis de mos' perty mornin' I ever see'd!"

The biscuits and the gravy didn't take no time at all to cook, but when I brung that plate to him his soul had flown away yonder. His face was all smiling, and he was looking out the window at the sun coming up in a glory of pinks and purples in the east.

I set down the tray and just climbed in beside of him and put my arms round him. And I watched the sunrise and knowed that this was my pappy's Great Gettin' Up Mornin'. In the light and color of that dawn I swear I could see a young Dimmy, tall and straight and all aglow, walking on up those clouds, and his mama there with her arms wide to greet him. I seen this, though most folks think I'm crazy when I tell of it.

So the old man left the troubles of this world behind, but he left me behind too.

I must have fell asleep there beside him. When I waked up Hezikiah were standing over the both of us and my dear Dimmy were cold as a stone.

"Uncle Dimmy has died, young Jim," Hez said.

"I know it," I told him and I got up.

Hez moaned and sat down hard in the willow rocker. He hung his head in his hands and were a pitiful sight.

I laid Uncle Dimmy out straight on the bed, covered him with a quilt, and sent to fetch the undertaker. Then we set down and Hez said some fine words about Uncle Dimmy and how today marked the end of lots of good things.

I did not say so, but I was thinking that this was a day Uncle Dimmy had been looking forward to for a long time and that for him it meant a new beginning. And it was the same for me. I had me a name and I had me an inheritance and a plan. Like the Hebrew children, I was about to depart from the land of Pharaoh Trueblood forevermore.

"Where are you and Mizz Nancy goin'?" I asked Hez while we waited.

"West. I've got a little money saved. I've got my own team and a wagon. Trueblood don't own everything. We'll head to St. Joseph first, and then come spring we'll make for California." His eyes was real sorrowful when he looked at me. "Wish we could take you with us, Jim."

"Don't worry yourself, Mister Hez. I'll be fine."

"I want you to know that me and Nancy talked it over long time back. If this trouble ain't come about the will and such, me and Nancy had meant to set y'all free . . . both you and Uncle Dimmy when the propity come into our hands. But it weren't meant to be. Uncle Dimmy died a slave."

"Well, he be free now, Mister Hez," I told him. All the while I was thinking how I was going to be free soon too.

"So he is."

"I'd rather be Uncle Dimmy. Rather live a good life like he done, than be rich like old Trueblood when he tries to pass through them Pearly Gates."

Chapter 4

The funeral come off just like Uncle Dimmy pictured it in his mind. Old man Trueblood spoke harsh words to the undertaker about it. He said Uncle Dimmy weren't nothing but an old nigger slave and that it was a waste of money to send off a nigger in such a way. Trueblood claimed that Dimmy's money belonged to the freight company and to Trueblood. That undertaker just give Trueblood a long solemn look like he was measuring him for a coffin.

"The late Uncle Dimmy saved his funds for years in anticipation of the occasion of his demise. I know it and so does everyone in Flora who contributed to the send-off."

To make a long story short, Trueblood did not manage to wheedle even one cent out of the undertaker. There were six prancing horses with plumes; a brass band; and me wearing top hat and boiled shirt and riding atop a carriage. It was real fine. The preacher preached a real good send-off, then the white folks went home and all of us folks went on back to our church and you might say we devoured the fatted calf in Dimmy's honor!

I hardly ever had such a feast in my life! It was announced that Uncle Dimmy, always thinking ahead, had bought up Fanny Brown's whole litter of weanling pigs for the event. We coloreds had us pit barbecue pork and catfish cooked up the way Dimmy liked it. Makes my mouth water to think on it even now. I suspect that the white folks of Flora was sorry they could not join us that day! We sung and there was more hallelujah preaching and everybody gave testimony on into the night. Oh glory! What a day!

And then it were over and we danced home by lantern light. I didn't feel sorrow no more. I sat opposite to that willow rocker and I told Dimmy thanks for everything and what a good time everybody had.

I talked to that empty chair quite a bit for the next few days.

Everybody were run off from the barn but me and the livestock. Mister Trueblood fired the stable hand. Of course Hez and Mizz Nancy was long gone. I stayed there working alone, cleaning the stalls and feeding the critters and mending the corral gate whilst I thought about my gold double eagles and hoped nothing bad would happen before I could tell Sam my plan.

On Monday morning Mister Trueblood hobbled in with the town constable at his side. Constable Hobbs was shame-faced so I knowed something was up. He had leg irons in his hand. I was raking up straw and I looked up and leaned on the handle and smiled real friendly, like I hadn't noticed them leg irons.

"How're you gettin' on?" the constable asked me. He shuffled his right foot in the dirt.

"Right fine," I answered. "Mister Trueblood, you looking well."

Trueblood scowled and spat. "I figgered ye to be gone. Figgered ye'd hightail it outta here."

I did not look at them irons. "Where would I go, Mister Trueblood? Everybody in Flora knows I got no life but this. Got these critters to tend and I done took over all of Uncle Dimmy's room. Got the bed all to myself now. Ain't that fine?"

Trueblood's lower lip stuck out. His eyes got real skinny and mean. "Happy here, are ye?"

"Right happy, Mister Trueblood. Real glad that freeman got hisself fired. It bothered me some to have him doing my chores."

This seemed to satisfy Trueblood. He mumbled to the constable that maybe they wouldn't be needing to restrain me. All this time I was thinking about Sam and that riverboat stopping at the levy the next day. I was sweating whilst I was playing dumb and smiling like a fool.

Trueblood cleared his throat. Constable Hobbs looked relieved. He put the chains behind his back.

Trueblood turned on his heel and said as he walked out, "I've hired me a business manager for Green Freight Company. Expect him soon from St. Louis."

They left me then, but I could still hear the clank of them irons. I knowed that I did not have much time and that I had better make good my escape the first time or nothing could free me except I go by the way of the grave, like Uncle Dimmy.

That night I stayed up talking to the willow chair and to the Lord about my freedom. I prayed that Sam would come on back here, even if he had heard that the Tack Room

Restaurant was closed down and that there wouldn't be no icing to lick from the bowl nor chicken to eat.

By the time the morning come I was altogether done in. All the same, for fear Trueblood would come back, I took to my chores. I fed the horses and the mules and polished the tack, saddles, and such. Just the same stuff that I done since the day Hez took me onto a riverboat and brung me here. I picked up the first saddle I ever cleaned and remembered how my hands was blistered when I finished. Now my hands was strong and tough. I could jerk down half a ton of misbehaving mule with one arm. I could drive an eight-up team hauling three freight wagons. Mister Trueblood had got a bargain in me after all, hadn't he? I had earned my keep a thousand times over.

It come to me then that if Sam did not come that day I would steal Redman, Trueblood's racing horse and the fastest horse in Missouri. I figured that if I was going to get hung for being a horse thief, it might as well be for stealing the best horse. Then I begun singing that old hymn, "Steal Away to Jesus."

By verse three I was most sure of what I was going to do. Then I heard the hinges groan on the barn door and I looked up. There stood Sam in his blue apprentice river pilot coat and his cap. He was toting a bundle in a carpetbag.

I stopped singing, right glad he had come, but not so desperate to see him now that I had a second plan.

"Howdy, Mister Sam," I said to him right cheerful.

"Well, this is a fine thing." He looked around at the emptiness. "Nothing for me to eat?"

"Not unless you want to share a feedbag with Redman."

He come on in and climbed up on the top rail of the stall to watch me curry Redman. I didn't talk about what all had happened, but he knowed it all anyway.

"So things have gone sour."

"A mite."

"Old Trueblood tossed everyone out?"

"Everyone but Dimmy. Dimmy flew away and I'm left."

"You staying?"

"I ain't been sold down the river yet, if you know what I mean."

Sam had a sly look in his eye. "Uncle Dimmy had a word with me about you before he passed on."

"Is 'at so?"

Sam looked over his shoulder and crooked his finger for me to come closer so as nobody could hear him. He dug into his pocket and pulled out a shiny double eagle gold piece. "Your Uncle Dimmy gave this to me. He said that there would be another for me if I helped you go north. News of the old man's demise and the closing of the Tack Room is all up and down the river. I thought I should keep my promise to him about you. We had figgered to get you on board the *Mary Belle* by pretending to take you to visit your mama. Then you were supposed to fall overboard or some such thing, and I'd come on back to Flora and tell everyone you drowned."

I was surprised at all this. I did not figure that an escape had been discussed before time.

"Y'all is something, Pappy," I spoke to Uncle Dimmy and that great cloud of witnesses who was watching this. Then I said to Sam, "It might have worked last week. But Trueblood is on the warpath."

Sam tossed his bundle onto the haystack. "I brought you a present." He was grinning big and motioned his head at the carpetbag. "Open it."

Inside that bag was a new suit of white man's clothes and new shoes big enough to fit me. Along with that was a bowler hat, round spectacles, a light brown wig, a bottle of bayrhum toilet water to make me smell like a Mississippi gambler, and face paint that Sam had bought off a lewd woman in St. Louis.

"Shave close. Smear this greasepaint on your face. It'll lighten your skin enough so you'll look and smell like a dandy off to see the sights. Not even your own dog will know you. You'll walk onto the *Mary Belle* at my side and . . ." He clouded. "You have that other double eagle? And expenses?" He named off the cost of the clothes and the wig and the face paint. I told him I could meet the price.

He was satisfied. "The *Mary Belle* is headed north today. If it all comes off, you'll be free by Sunday!"

I thought about New Orleans and how I wanted to go and see my mama. Sam saw the thought go through my head. He told me to forget it because in the far-off chance that anyone did think about me going south, they might remember my mama was there and send the law to question her. The only thing to do was to head north, as far from Flora as I could get, beyond St. Louis and all the way up to Iowa.

"Get dressed," he said. "I'm going to eat down at Flora's Restaurant as my alibi, and then I'll wait at the back stairs of the hotel. You meet me there."

I done all that I was told. I shaved and doused myself with bayrhum so as not even Lester Smith's prize bluetick hound would have knowed my scent. I dug up my gold pieces and put them in a sock and tied it round my neck. Then I dressed up in all that St. Louis finery and put my feet into them fine patent leather shoes. Wig, greasepaint, and powder come next, and finally the spectacles. I looked in the looking glass, but hardly knowed myself. Even so, I was feeling half sick with the fear that somebody might spot me. I looked at my hands and knowed what Sam had forgot. I needed a pair of gloves!

I was figuring what to do when I heard footsteps behind of me. I turned around and there was Old Mister Trueblood and another fella who I did not know. I plunged my hands in my pockets and acted like I was admiring Redman.

Trueblood hollered past me, "Jim! Where are you? Jim! You sleepin' in the hayloft? Get down here, lazy no-good! I've brought your new boss!"

His weak old eyes was just glaring with fury. He cursed his slave Jim as if it weren't me at all. Then he stared right at me and I seen he didn't know who I was.

I lowered my voice and put on a deep southern accent. "Nobody heah, Mistah. Ah heard y'all had the fastest hoss in Missouri in this barn and ah figgered to have m'self a look whilst the rivuhboat was stopped. This must be that hoss. There ain't nobody in this barn but me," I told Trueblood.

At this, old Trueblood started sputtering and turning shades of red into purple. He blasphemed something terrible and begun to shout that his nigger had run away! He said most likely that shiftless no-good had stole a horse and took to his heels in the night. Probably that Jim had run off to find Hezikiah Green and make good an escape to California where they would open a cafe!

Now the fella beside Trueblood had never seen me as a stable hand. For all he knowed, I was just what I looked to be—a gambler come to look at a horse. The three of us walked out together and I said to both of them how terrible it was that the old gentleman's stable boy had lit out like that. I told them how once my daddy in Natchez had a pair of slaves who lit out together because they was wearing leg irons and how they fell into a pond only six feet deep and drowned because of the irons.

It was a fine story. It set old Trueblood off on how he almost put that no-good Jim in leg irons, but the constable had talked him out of it because he thought Jim was too dumb to run.

Trueblood was apoplectic. I was hoping he'd turn to stone and drop dead just like old King Herod in the Good Book. He waved his cane like a sword, and I remembered the first time he beat me with that cane and then the last time he done it, and I had to calm myself because it got me riled inside all over again. Not looking back, I strolled beside the new fella until we turned the corner toward the back of the hotel.

There was Sam, smoking a pipe and standing on the step. He looked up at the three of us coming at him, and then he looked away because he still hadn't seen that it was me. Then he coughed on the tobacco smoke and looked back in wonder that I was walking beside old Trueblood and clucking my tongue and telling him that he would surely catch his nigger by and by.

"Howdy, Sam!" I said real big.

"Hey, James!" he said back to me.

"This poor gent has a runaway slave," I said in my deep voice.

Sam joined the chorus of sympathy. I made as if to walk on with Trueblood and the new man, but Sam caught me by the arm. "We'll miss the boat, James," he said to me. "She's due to cast off in five minutes. I thought you'd never come." Then he tipped his hat to Trueblood and bade them a fine farewell, wishing them good luck with the runaway. We went in the back door of the hotel, through the lobby, and out the front door.

From there it was the longest walk I ever took in my born days, even though it weren't but a block to the boat. I kept my hands down in my pockets. My knees was shaking. Me and Sam strolled easy like on down the street past folks I had known for years. Sam was talking all the while about the price of cotton and the weather and such. Nobody looked twice at me. Together, me and Sam climbed up the gangway. I set myself down in a wicker chair on the deck and pulled my hat down over my eyes and pretended to doze whilst the *Mary Belle* cast off and the big wheel begun to churn upriver toward the North and freedom. I count that moment as the real beginning of my life.

------◆•◆•◆------

I stayed on deck until the *Mary Belle* was an hour out of Flora. A strong wind swooped down from the north and the skies clouded over. It was dark as night, even though it was the middle of the afternoon. The lightning begun to flash, and the thunder rolled over us like a bass drum. It begun to pour down rain—fierce and mean it streamed down—carving little rivulets in the clay of the river banks and nibbling away the levies. If it weren't for fear of washing the greasepaint off my face, I would have stood out in it and let it baptize me in the pure water of freedom!

It come to me that even if I got caught by the bounty man and hung from a tree, this one day would be worth dying for. I never felt so fine as that afternoon watching the lightning bolts split the dark sky and strike earth and water all around us!

Some on board that riverboat was scared that we would be hit, but I had no such fear. It felt like the Almighty Himself put on a show just for me on the day of my jubilee. A kind of celebration it was, and more than that.

Some may doubt my word, but I am telling the truth. As I watched and listened to the thunder, I plainly heard a voice of great and terrible wrath, of things that would come upon the North and South. I seen a terrible vision of blood and glory in the lightning that day.

Later, when the war come and the nation finally split in two, I was not surprised by it, for I knowed from that day on the *Mary Belle* that it was coming like a mighty storm.

I was the only passenger who did not beat a path into the main salon or into a sleeping cabin. Night had come by the time Sam found me out on deck. He looked surprised to see me still in the deck chair like he had forgot where he put me. He told me to get up and follow him, which I done. He led me down the stairs to a small sleeping cabin on the lower deck and told me I should get in there and not show my face until he said I could come out. He brung me a red flannel nightshirt and said he would bring me my grub morning and night. If anyone else come by and knocked, I was to make like I was sick, and say I wanted to be left to myself.

So I done what he said. In the daylight hours I slept in the cabin. Sam brung me plenty to eat and emptied my chamber pot. When night come and the white folks gambled and danced and caroused in the fancy salon, I sneaked outside and stood in the blackness by the rail from time to time. Nobody noticed me there and Sam never knowed I done it. I watched the lights of little river towns slide on by, and I studied on all the folks in them towns like me who would soon be free and all the young men who would die trying to hold them captive. The vision had showed me these things, and I never doubted that war was coming.

In this way the time on the *Mary Belle* passed quickly for me. We come to St. Louis and moored up among fifty other paddle wheelers on the quay. Passengers left and around noon Sam stopped by my cabin with word that the Mississippi had rose so high that the levies was near to breaking and the rain was still pouring.

"We're going to take on fuel and head right out. We'll be evacuating women and children all along the way north no doubt."

It was plain to see that he was nervous on account of helping me get away from Trueblood. The strain was beginning to wear on him. Soon enough the riverboat would be full of folks, women and youngins in need of shelter, and yet here I hid with a cabin all to myself. Other menfolk traveling on the *Mary Belle* had already removed their traps from their cabins to get ready for the folks going to be evacuated.

I looked out the round window and there stood the city of St. Louis; all brick and stone and fine buildings with tall smokestacks.

"I have a notion that I don't want to go no further north without seeing St. Louis first," I said to Sam.

"Are you crazy? I figured to take you all the way to Iowa. Dubuque. Iowa's a free state. Even with the fugitive slave laws, folks don't take kindly to the bounty hunters there. They don't give those fellas any help with their dirty business. Iowa's a safe place to settle."

"I fancy seeing St. Louis, myself."

"I couldn't let you go without saying that half the folks in Missouri still own slaves. This is a border state, Jim. You still aren't a freeman here."

"I aim to see St. Louis." I put on my starched shirt front and my suit coat. "You done carried me as far as I aim to go."

Sam studied me for a moment to see if I was in earnest about my plan.

"I see you mean to do this thing, although I think you are a pure fool for it."

"I'll buy me a team of mules and a freight wagon here in St. Louis and drive myself north to Iowa. Nobody gonna stop me, even though I ain't white. When I be driving a team of mules, no bounty man looks twice. I done it a thousand times for Green Freight Company and nobody ever stopped me and asked my business whilst I got a team in my hands. The bounty man will be looking for some ragged, footsore scarecrow flapping through the brush toward the North. Hide in plain sight; that is my intention."

Sam did not know that my knees was shaking when I

got ready to leave him at the docks in St. Louis. I figured that by getting off the *Mary Belle* whilst she was still in Missouri, it would be less likely that the bounty man could pin anything on Sam if the question of my disappearance should ever come up. A white man could go to prison for helping a slave get free. That was the law of them days and Sam had broke it for me. He had risked enough already, and I knowed that he had not done this for me only on account of the money.

He shook my hand the way one freeman does with another; like equals. I felt mighty proud to know him. I would say that Sam was my first real friend, though he was white and me colored.

He wished me good luck and Godspeed on my journey and told me that he felt sure since I had made it this far, that I would make it all the way to freedom in safety. When we said farewell, I did not figure I would ever see him again.

I did not wear greasepaint to cover the color of my skin that day. Even so, I kept them specs in my pocket in case I should see someone from Flora who might be in St. Louis.

I felt mighty sorrowful when I turned around and waved one last time to Sam. I might have been on the road to freedom, but that did not change the fact that it would be a lonely road for many a year.

Chapter 5

It was the summer of '61. The War between the States had yet to amount to much. The rebs had took that fort down South Carolina way. Some battles had got fought, and some young men had got theirselves killed, but most everybody up north was certain that it would get over double quick, once it got rolling.

Then, in July, the secesh whipped the boys in blue at a place they called Manassas. It made Old Abe's generals take a long, hard look at the thing, kind of rethinking it all. Both sides settled down to growling at each other across the Virginia line and that's the way she sat. Except in Missouri, worse luck, right where I was about to be smack in the middle.

Folks in Missouri weren't clear for one side nor the other, and tempers boiled as high as the July sun baking down on the dirt roads. Both North and South allowed as how they would have Missouri and no two ways about it. Union soldiers plumped down in St. Louis, and when they declined Governor Jackson's request to leave, he made a fire-eating speech and called them invaders. He give a call for fifty thousand men to join up in militia and throw the

Yankee soldiers out, and that sure enough stirred the fire under the powder keg.

I had me a wagon and a brace of mules, and I was making out pretty fair, hiring on to cart folks' stuff, hauling firewood and the like. At the time I was living in Keokuk, that corner of Iowa that snuggles up next to Missouri. I was most trying to ignore the war and carry on with my business when it jumped up and bit me.

I got a contract to haul supplies for the Union boys. Seems they were headed down the Mississippi, digging out rebels as they went. To go along weren't exactly my decision, neither. They said they needed the use of my rig, with or without me. That made up my mind for me, and the next thing I knowed, I was in a line of wagons heading south.

For a long time we didn't see no rebels to speak of. Sometimes a lean, hollow-cheeked, proud-eyed farmer would lean over his rail fence and spit louder than necessary when the soldiers went by. But for most of two weeks we traipsed from place to place, always hearing about a pack of rebels here and a band of raiders there, but never catching hold of any what would hold still to be shot at. I believe it had something to do with what General Lyon caused to be tacked up on the trees all around: yellow playbill-sized notes what said that anyone caught bearing arms against the United States government would be hanged as a traitor. Kind of took the glamour out of the vision.

Then late one afternoon, we come upon an old sugar maple camp. It had not been used for a great many years, but there was signs all around that a bunch of men had stayed there and left not long before. There was still a hand-ful of grain in the splintered sugar trough from where they fed their horses, and hollowed-out places in the dirt inside the corncrib showed where twelve or fifteen had been sleeping.

The colonel, man named Grant—him that was later general and then president—said that the rebels was right close and the men should look sharp. He got word from his scouts that the trail led toward a farm not more than three miles away. He figured to creep up on the farm in the dark. Just at daybreak, when there was light enough so as not to shoot friends, they'd pounce on that nest and bag the lot.

I weren't no soldier and didn't carry no gun. So it was just fine with me when a captain told us teamsters to stay at the old sugar camp 'til morning. He left us in the charge of a sergeant, a red-faced Irishman who swore something colorful, and all them soldier boys went off sneaking through the brush.

Long about midnight, I was under my wagon sleeping when something woke me up. At first I couldn't make out what had roused me. Then I heard a noise, a low cough, just up a brushy ravine from where we was. A minute later and I heard it again.

I crawled over to the corncrib on my belly and shook the sergeant awake. "Sergeant," I said, "there's somebody up that little canyon back of us."

He grunted and snorted like a steam engine pulling up a grade, and presently he went to cussing me in a voice that probably carried clear to St. Louis. "What are you waking me up for, you no-good . . ." and me trying to shush him.

Instead of getting quiet, he got louder, what with telling me at the top of his lungs that even a wooly-headed nigger like me shouldn't be scared of some old cow out in the woods.

Well, about the time the sergeant had cussed his way back five generations of my family, a raspy voice yells "Charge!" and a pack of rebels came whooping and hollering out of the canyon.

The sergeant fumbled a Colt Army out of a holster hanging from a nail over his head and managed to drop the thing. It went off with a roar and then the party really got rolling.

"Form a line!" the raspy voice called out and then "Fire!" A half dozen muskets went off pretty close together. A mule got hit and give an unearthly scream, and a couple of lead balls whizzed through both sides of the corncrib just over my head. Outside, I heard the other mule skinners tearing off into the woods.

The sergeant didn't even wait to try to locate his pistol. He crashed headfirst into the wall away from the rebs and busted out just like a bull. I couldn't think of nothing better to do than follow his example, so I snaked through the opening he made and took to my heels.

But my livelihood, my team and wagon, was back there by that camp. So after doing a hundred yards in the dark, I slid to a stop behind a clump of soapberry bushes to catch my breath and figure out how to go back after my belongings. The rebs could have the supplies for all I cared, but I really needed that team.

I found the bottom end of the same gully that pointed back toward the maple camp and I crept up as quiet as a mouse. I calculated on being able to get my mules at least, on account of I had picketed them a little ways off from the camp where a little seep of water had raised a patch of grass.

When I got close again, I could hear that same grating voice ordering men to hurry. He was after them to round up the stock and all the equipment they could, especially guns and ammunition. The farm folks thereabouts would feed southern militiamen for free, so they did not need the cornmeal, but their weapons were few and of poor quality, and they prized the mules.

Working myself around to the east, I come to the clearing where I had staked the team, when a regular bust-all broke out again. From the shots fired and the angry yells, I guessed that the federal soldiers had just been right behind the rebs and had jumped them in turn just as they had jumped us.

It weren't going to get any quieter, so I sprinted toward the mules, unfolding a Barlow knife as I ran. I figured to slash the picket line, not slowing to even pull the pin, let alone untie the knot. Them mules was already most skittish from the musket fire popping around, because when I come up under Shadrach's nose, he reared back and busted the tether.

"Whoa, boy," I said, trying to keep it low and make him mind at the same time. But Shadrach, he weren't having none of it. I made a grab for the scrap of rope trailing from his headstall, and he reared again and spun me half round from a swipe of his hoof. He clattered off into the blackness, leaving me feeling stupid and fearful I might still come up empty.

Meshach was tethered on the other side of the clearing. I couldn't see him exactly, except for the flash of a white blaze on his face. "Easy, Meshach," I called out to him, friendly like. "Just me. Don't be scared." That didn't even sound convincing to me, because no more than two hundred yards away the rifle fire was still rattling and everybody yelling at once.

I got my hand on the rope alright. He was a sure enough tall mule, but I was a big man and I reached up my arm and grabbed him around the neck. Then I cut the line gentlelike so as not to spook him.

Thinking I had it made, I went to lead him off at a fast walk, toward the southeast away from the fight. That's when something slapped him on the rump. I heard it plain as day. His head whipped around like a snake striking, with me holding on and my feet flying through the air. I had no time to give it thought right then, but it must have been a spent rifle ball that come sailing through the trees and give him a whack.

I might still have wrestled him down, but just as he was slinging me around like I was a rat in a bulldog's mouth, I come face-to-face with somebody who that very second broke free of the brush. I do mean face-to-face too. Our skulls bashed together. The fella gave a groan and fell down like a hog knocked on the head with a sledgehammer.

I weren't far behind neither. I stared for a minute at a thin gleam of moonlight shining on the blade of the folding knife still clutched in my hand. Then the ground of them Missouri woods opened up and swallowed me, and down into the brush I crashed.

The morning sun was warm on the back of my neck. I could hear a mockingbird yelling "Get up! Get up!" but when I made to rouse myself and look around I got a fierce pain over my eyes and I squinched them both tight shut again. I thought how I'd just go on laying in the brush awhile longer, before aiming to see.

Trying to sort out what had happened the previous night and how I come to be where I was, I didn't pay no mind to a little rustle in the grass down by my feet. The second time it come, I had to pay closer attention, because something slid up across my leg.

Now I've always heard that if a snake gets on you, you should lay real still 'til he gets tired and goes on about his business somewheres else. People what says such foolishness have never had a cottonmouth chase them cross a pond.

I jumped six feet long and four high, just like a jackrabbit. When I lighted again, I grabbed up the first stout branch that come to hand and whirled around to thrash that snake for frighting me so.

That sun was powerful bright! So peering first through one squinted eye and then the other, I raised my club and kind of sidled back toward the spot.

It weren't no snake at all! There was a man laying there! He was squirming and rustling around and had throwed his arm over my leg. Then it all come back to me with a rush; how I'd most nearly got clear with Meshach 'til crashing into somebody. This had to be that self-same fella. Since he didn't have no uniform on, just a little gray cap laying beside him, he was one of the rebel bunch.

Keeping the tree branch at the ready in case he come to feeling as rough as me, I called out to him. "Mister . . . wake up. You ain't dead, I reckon."

He shook a head full of brown, curly hair and groaned.

Then, after two tries, he pushed himself up on one elbow and rolled half over. "Mister Sam!" I said, startled when I seen who it was. "It's Jim. Jim Canfield. What are you doing out here?"

In a real dry tone he says, "I could ask you the same thing, couldn't I, Jim? Was that your mule that kicked me last night?"

"It sure enough was," I lied. What with the blood dried on his forehead, it didn't seem the right time to tell what really happened. "I'm powerful sorry. You alright?"

"I will be when my size twelve head quits feeling like it's crammed into a size six hat."

He sat up, rubbing a lump on his noggin the size of a goose egg. I told him how I come to be out in the Missouri woods and then he explained his part to me.

"Marion Rangers," he said with a snort and a careful shake of his head. "We must be the most expert bunch of soldiers in the military maneuver of retreating in the whole of the Confederate cause. All we've done for the past three weeks is fall back, retreat, withdraw, and fall back again. We would have carried out our twenty-second successful retreat last night if it hadn't been for that new Captain Clayton."

"Him with the voice like a file rounding off a horse-shoe?"

Sam nodded in agreement. "That's the one. Got the bright idea to outflank the federal army boys and seize the supplies. Wonder if anybody got killed?" Then his forehead creased with more than just pain. "I'm not going back," he said. "I'm going home. I only joined up because all my friends did. But you know I don't hold with slavery Jim, nor secession either. Last night, blasting away in the dark like that, I might have gotten killed, or killed somebody . . . might have even shot you. I'm through playing soldier."

"That's good, Mister Sam," I agreed. "We can head out together. I'm living in Keokuk. Got me a business . . . or did have 'til I lost my team and wagon last night."

"Keokuk, eh? My brother lives in Keokuk." He stood up and wavered a little like a pine swaying in a high wind, putting his hand up to his head.

"Just set down again for a minute," I said, and I tore a strip off my shirttail. I soaked the rag in water from the seep of the spring and tied it slantways across his head. He said it helped some, even if the moisture did open the split a mite. A spot of blood the size of a half-dollar soaked through the cloth.

"Your mules are smarter than us," Sam said. "I bet they left for home last night . . . probably halfway there by now. Maybe we'll catch up with them. Let's just get clear away from here so nobody decides to shoot at us."

Leaning together, we looked like an old A-frame shanty where one wall holds up the other. We navigated north by the sun until we come to a road and got our bearings. Climbing a small knoll, we kept to a ridge of high ground where we could watch out for other folks and my mules too.

By and by, we caught the sound of wood-chopping coming from a bowl-shaped hollow up ahead. The dip in the earth was ringed by trees and we couldn't see down into it, but the noise of firewood being split had a homey sort of sound, peaceful-like and untroubled. Not warlike at all. Besides, Sam and me reckoned it was bad enough to miss breakfast with no remedy, so we didn't plan to miss dinner too if it could be helped. We swung down into that hollow, busting through branches and making all kinds of racket.

A half-dozen grim-looking rebels popped out of nowhere all around us. Their hair and beards was scraggly and their guns nought but squirrel rifles, but they were convincing enough: we walked nice and easy down to their camp.

The leader was a brute of a man with coal black hair down to his shoulders and a curly black beard all mixed up with a mat of chest hair that overflowed his flannel shirt. He was as tall as me but half again as heavy as my two hundred pounds. He seen us being brought in, but before he comes over he says to another bunch of three fellas, "Go on with your practicin'."

Mister Sam's eyes most bugged out of his head when he seen what their practice was. The sound we had took for chopping kindling was made by bowie knives full thirty inches long. Them men was swinging two handed, hacking great chunks out of a tree stump. I seen that the leader had one of them blades hanging from his belt like a sword.

"Who are yuh and what are yuh doin' here?" he demanded.

Now this didn't look like no time to say that I had been hauling freight for the Yankee army, and Sam, he was tongue-tied on account of he was a deserter from the same side these folks was with.

I put on my slowest fieldhand drawl, so as to sound like I come from the deep South. "Please, cap'n, suh," I said real respectful-like. "Dem Yankee so'jers clubbed massa and took de wagon. Kin you he'p us, suh?"

All at once he was just as friendly as he had been fierce before. He took Sam over to his shelter (though it weren't but a brush arbor built over willow poles). He sat Sam down on a three-legged stool and fussed over my bandaging job with clumsy, sausage-shaped fingers. Then they fed us both plates of catfish and corn pone and offered to recruit Sam into their outfit.

A new alarm was raised with the cry of "Horseman comin'!" There was an exchange of signs and countersigns, and then the newcomer was allowed to ride right straight up to the fire. "Greetings, Colonel Pike," said a slick little man in a city suit and an elegant pair of tall, shiny boots. "Captain Abner Grimes at your service. My compliments to your organization. General Tom Harris requests that your men be ready to join with his in an action down near Springfield within the week."

Pike, with his heft and brawn, looked more like a country blacksmith than anything I ever saw called colonel down New Orleans way. He stood up and pulled that two and a half feet of knife out of his belt. He swept it across in front of him, then brought it up to his shoulder in salute, as if he were wearing gold braid on a parade ground.

"Tell the gen'rl, we'll be thar," Pike promised.

"And who might these be?" asked the smart-dressed fella, staring at me and Sam.

"This gentleman an' his boy was set upon by Yankees," Pike offered for us. "We're just patchin' them up some an' fillin' their bellies 'fore we send 'em along home."

I didn't like the look that horseman give us. His eyes got real narrow and suspicious and he smoothed his blonde moustache. "Do you think that's wise, Colonel? Yankee spies have been operating hereabouts and now these two know the location of your camp."

Pike looked doubtful and things might have gone bad for us if Sam had not found his voice at last. "I resent the implication, sir!" he said, jumping up from the stool. "I have sustained a wound, an honorable wound, in combat with the enemy, and suffered serious deprivation of property in the encounter. I do not see any such marks on you . . . how have you suffered for the cause? I demand your immediate apology!"

A growl of approval came from Pike at this statement. The dapper man raised an eyebrow and tilted his head to the side. "I meant no offense," he said at last. "These are perilous times to be sure, and one cannot be too cautious. Now I must be off to other encampments."

I was right glad that when Grimes headed out he went away south, direct opposite to us. Sam said good-bye to Colonel Pike, declining once more the offer of a commission with his group. Pike said he liked Sam's spirit and that his tone would add some class to the company. But even the promise of high times to come down Springfield way could not induce Sam to stay, so he thanked Pike for the hospitality and we pushed off.

Walking all the rest of that day, we slept in a barn, then rose at dawn the next morning to put some more miles between us and the recent skirmish. We was just outside of Hannibal, which was the town Sam called home, when a young U.S. cavalry officer in a dusty blue uniform clattered up with a detachment of horsemen. He demanded to know our business and where we was going.

Sam said, truthfully enough, that we were headed for

Keokuk. He added that his brother lived there and that I had a business there.

"How did you come by that head wound?" the officer inquired. "It looks like a bullet grazed you. Have you been in a fight?"

Sam laughed and touched the bandage. "Total stranger got mad when I told him the secesh rebels are traitors to their country. Hit me with a chunk of stovewood and made some unkind remarks about my partner Jim here."

Partner! That clinched it for the soldier boy. No secesh would call a mulatter his partner. "Mind you get on your way then," the lieutenant urged. "There are roving bands of rebel militia accosting travelers after dark."

"You don't say," Sam said. "Can anything be done about it?"

"Certainly," laughed the young officer. "We hanged a pair of snipers in Hannibal yesterday. Belonged to some guerilla outfit . . . rangers or something. We mean to string up some more, soon as we catch them."

Sam shuddered as the detail rode away. I knew he was picturing the same things as me: some men swinging two-handed bowie knives and other men swinging from the ends of ropes. "Well, partner," he said at last, "I don't think Keokuk is far enough from Missouri to suit me, but it's a good start."

Chapter 6

Sam's older brother Orion had him a law office in Keo-kuk. That is to say, he had a rolltop desk beside a window and a row of law books over the fireplace mantle in a little downstairs parlor. The two-story, pale yellow clapboard house where this parlor was located actually belonged to his wife's ma and pa.

Sam always said that Orion was the most honest and truthful fellow what ever lived, and that such character traits was a defect in a practicer of the legal profession, to quote him more or less. Said Orion was so able to see both sides of an issue that by the time he got done defending a man, even his client would have voted "guilty." Sam said this broad-mindedness was why Orion's law firm didn't have any business to speak of, and why him and his wife and their little girl didn't have a place of their own.

Orion was a fine-looking man, square jawed, to my mind favoring Colonel Grant as to his face and neat trimmed brown beard. He was a soft-spoken man who always treated me square and never seemed to get into the kind of scrapes that Sam fell over just by walking down the street. Any troubles Orion run into come from believing any old outlandish tale. Sam said, and I seen it myself, that his brother was the single most gullible man on the planet.

When we got to the house, Orion was acting excited, pacing up and down in front of the fireplace and wringing his hands. Sam tried to tell him the story of the Battle of the Sugar Camp, no doubt expecting to puff up his part some, but Orion had a story of his own to tell.

"It's come, Sam," he said with a satisfied sound in his voice. "You said it would never amount to anything, but here it is for real. All that time I put in stumping for Bates's election in the last campaign is finally going to pay off."

I guessed from the look on his face that Sam had heard his brother get worked up over things before. Sam told me that Orion was always helping out folks for free, instead of charging, and that everyone thought of Orion as an easy mark when they needed a loan to back some harebrained scheme or other. I saw that Sam was having thoughts such as these when his brother continued.

"Bates has joined Lincoln's Cabinet. One of the positions in his patronage is secretary, and he's offered it to me."

Sam's jaw dropped! "Secretary of what? You can't mean in Lincoln's government. Do you mean undersecretary? Of what? Treasury? Or do you mean private secretary for Bates?"

Orion got the biggest grin across his face. I could tell he was going to play this moment for all it was worth, probably because he didn't manage to impress his brother very often. He waited 'til Sam had loaded and fired a whole salvo of questions before he answered. "Grander than any of those! I am to be the secretary for . . ." he drew himself up on his toes and thrust his hand under his jacket in a right distinguished pose, "the Territory of Nevada!"

Letting fly a blast of air like a blacksmith's bellows, Sam give out with a single laugh. He sat down and laughed still more, and wrapped his arms around his ribs, as if he figured that laughing so hard would bust something loose. "Nevada!" he said at last, when he caught his breath. "Secretary to a hunk of desert that has more Indians than white folks? What will you report on, Mister Secretary? The condition of this year's crop of sagebrush? The alarming invasion of horned toads?"

Orion looked right taken down a peg. He tried to give it back to Mister Sam, but it was halfhearted at best. "It is a terrific opportunity! You have heard of the huge silver strike, haven't you? It's like the gold rush of '49 all over again. Thousands moving there, striking it rich! Why it'll be a state in no time! I could grow up with it, maybe be governor some day!"

Sam growled, "Grow up is right! When they find more sand than silver in those holes in the ground, where will you be then? What about moving your family out to the desolate wilderness? Disease, savages, drought, wild animals . . ."

Easing down into a chair across the room from his brother, Orion's chin drooped on his chest and all the excitement seeped out of him like a pat of butter oozing over a plate in the summer heat.

It weren't my place to speak, but I just couldn't take no more. "Mister Sam, you did ought to let your brother tell you more before you go to bad-mouthing his chance. Go on, Mister Orion, tell us more. What do the job pay?"

Getting regular pay was not something that had often happened in Orion's past and my question struck the right tune with Sam. "Yes," he agreed. "Tell us what it pays."

"Eighteen hundred," Orion said simply.

"Dollars?"

Orion nodded once.

"A year?"

He nodded again. A man thought himself well paid if he took home five dollars a day. So eighteen hundred a year was not the riches of Solomon, but it was a substantial sum.

Sam looked astonished. "Well, I'll be . . . I owe you an apology, Orion. This sounds like it might be for real after all."

It was a wonder how much Orion's face brightened at them words. Ain't it amazing how much joy and how much sorrow can be caused by things as unsubstantial as words? Orion got back some of his enthusiasm. "And you can go with me," he said. "The job provides for me to have an assistant. I'll not try to bring Mary and Jenny out until I've built them a house. What do you say? Shall we be old bachelors together for a year or so?"

This offer was made so earnest and with such plain longing for approval that even Sam bit back the harsh words that I seen was straining his throat. "No," he said. "It's not for me. But thank you, Orion, for thinking of me."

There was a knock at the front door and Orion left to answer it, asking Sam and me not to leave yet and for Sam to think it over before deciding. Sam made a pouty face and shook his head at Orion's back; his mind was already made up. No desert for him, no sir! How our plans and God's do surely fall out with each other!

Orion came back into the parlor with a tall, rail-thin cadaver of a man. He had a hawk's beak for a nose and the deep-set, brooding eyes of an undertaker or maybe a hangman. Orion introduced him. "James Redpath, I'd like you to meet my brother Samuel and our friend Jim Canfield."

"How do you do?" Redpath said in a jovial voice that was far from matching his looks. He shook my hand before taking Sam's.

"Mister Redpath was one of John Brown's lieutenants," Orion said. "Now he is aiding the government in ferreting out rebels and traitors in Missouri. I have a letter here from Washington giving him extraordinary powers of arrest and trial."

"And find them I will," said Redpath cheerfully, as if daring anybody to argue. "I'll put a rope around every rebel's neck until they tell me all about their leaders . . . and when they have told me all, I'll haul them to the top of the tallest tree I can find, may God have mercy on their slave-abusing souls." He said this as happily as if he were talking about going varmint hunting or some other sport.

I heard Sam swallow hard. He muttered something about how evident was Redpath's dedication to duty or some such truck, and then he acted like he didn't trust hisself to say more. Orion fetched a letter from a pigeonhole of his desk and handed it to the abolitionist. "I wish you success," Orion said. "You may have heard that I am leaving these parts for my new position in the Territory of Nevada. No need for your services there, I imagine. No dangerous rebels in Nevada."

Redpath got a funny kind of crooked smile and said no,

he imagined not. With that, he shook hands around again and took his leave.

Most as soon as the door closed Sam was up and out of his chair. "Is that offer still good?" he asked, grabbing Orion's arm. "I feel an intense desire to see Nevada." As he said this he run his finger around the inside of his shirt collar as if it had right sudden got too tight for his throat.

———◆•◆•◆———

Sam invited me to come along to the new territory of Nevada. Never did find my mules, and of course the wagon was long gone, not that it would have made no difference without a team. Not having any business no more, nor any family in Keokuk, I couldn't see no reason not to go. It come to me that if I struck it rich, I could own a freight company entire, and if I busted I could still find work driving team for somebody else.

I think Mister Sam was grateful I said yes. He had remarked more than once that keeping an eye on Orion was a full-time job, and since Orion felt the exact same way about Sam, I was fairly nominated to play nursemaid to them both. Only three days went by between the time we made the acquaintance of Mister Redpath and the moment we left Keokuk to hook up with the westbound stage.

It was a hot, dry, dusty day when we took passage with the Overland Stage Company out of St. Joseph, Missouri, bound for Carson City, Nevada Territory. The fare was one hundred fifty dollars each, and nothing discounted for me having to ride outside the entire way on account of being black. I had only about half of that amount saved up, but Mister Sam paid the rest for me, saying I could pay him back out of the first shovelful of silver I dug up. He paid all of his brother's passage too, since Mister Orion didn't have no savings to speak of and the government didn't allow him no traveling funds.

The Concord coach had seats inside for six passengers, three looking forwards and three facing back. There was also little jump seats inside of the doors so the coach could haul eight inside at a pinch. Besides the driver, there was a conductor fella who rode up beside of him, and then on the roof of the whole affair they crammed as many other folks as could hang on, which included me.

That vehicle was pretty as a picture. It was sparkling clean, dark red trimmed, with yellow wheels and running gear. On the outside of both doors was a drawing of a right smart, Spanish-looking gal and the name "Esmeralda." Up on the box sat the driver, pulling on a long pair of new buckskin gloves, and never so much as sparing one look for the passengers nor the hostler standing at the head of the six-up team. The driver had a tall, shiny, stovepipe boot setting casual up on the brake and a coiled rawhide black-snake whip laying beside him on the seat.

Right then I got such a hankering to be a stage driver I thought I would die happy if ever I climbed to such a lofty position. I studied on it some waiting for Mister Sam and Mister Orion to get their baggage sorted out.

Neither one of them had reckoned on the fact that all you were allowed to take was twenty-five pounds of gear. Now that weren't no bother to me. After selling the little tack I had left from my freighting business, I could put all my worldly goods in what the old-timers called a "possibles" bag; about the size of a small carpet satchel.

But them two brothers! They had to unload all of two trunks and ship it back home. The conductor most laughed hisself silly watching them two dig out fancy dress suits and dancing pumps and such.

They managed to pare it down at last, and then their valises and my bag was throwed in the boot on top of about a half a ton of mail. The canvas cover was cinched down across the lot, and the passengers, which also included a lady and another gentleman, climbed aboard.

I climbed up behind of the driver, and then the conductor took his place. He looked at a big watch and give a little nod. That driver uncoiled his lash, and with a single crack of the whip the coach jumped forward and we was off; leaving the States behind and headed out on the first leg of a three-week journey that would carry us over two thousand miles.

Three-quarters of our travel passed without incident. We reached Nevada Territory and was winging along, skirting the Humboldt River. It was late twilight when we rolled into Warbonnet Station for a meal and to take on a new driver, or as they preferred to be called, jehu. Warbonnet was called a meal stop, but the only thing I found to eat was stone hard pone with no more than a handful of sand in each bite. The other fixings was fried bacon that was more white fuzz than pork and coffee made with well water already so brown that the ground-up Arbuckle beans seemed pointless.

The new driver, whose name was Frank, was of medium height and frame, with wide shoulders spreading a buffalo skin coat. He wore a broad-brimmed Texas hat above a blousy shirt and a wide leather belt topping buckskin breeches. His chin was stained from a mahogany dribble of tobacco juice. The old driver was bending Frank's ear about how some station keeper named Jules had got hisself fired; said Jules had been too loud once too often about how the South was going to whip the Yankees. Now Jules had turned renegade and was leading a band of northern Shoshones in raiding the stage line.

In an unnatural deep voice, the way a man will speak when he's trying to sound tough, Frank allowed that this fella Jules was a thief and a cutthroat on the run from the law. He said that none of them as fought for the Confederacy would welcome such as Jules.

Frank remarked that they was all better off now that Jules was give the get-along and that he expected to see Jules swinging from a gallows most any day. Our conductor said that if Frank talked much thataway, then he had best keep his six-shooter close to hand, as he was soon going to need it. That was all I heard before we commenced rolling again.

I didn't pay much mind, having heard rough talking folks before and knowing as a general thing that nothing ever come of it. Besides, the plains country was right pretty. A big, round, silver moon soared into the sky behind of us, and kind of swarmed upwards like the searchlight beam of a giant riverboat bent on overtaking our puny craft.

The light of heaven's lantern lit the open spaces 'til I could pick out rocks and scrawny bushes half a mile away. From my perch on top, I could hear the conductor and Frank talking in low tones. The sound of snores ripping out of the windows proved that Sam and Orion was sleeping.

I drifted off myself, lulled by the rocking of the coach on the leather straps called thoroughbraces when we pulled into another little station—just a corral and a lean-to hut, really—to change teams. Frank and the conductor had both got down for a minute while a skinny hostler swapped the horses for a six-up of mules. The conductor was back on the box and Frank was stepping up when somebody grabbed him from behind. Frank ripped off a string of swear words that would have raised the eyebrows of a mule skinner, and swung back around. That's when I heard him say "Jules!"

I heard a dull thud, like of a wooden club landing on flesh, and Frank give a cry of pain and then called out "Help!" Looking over the side of the coach, I seen one big, bearded ruffian swinging a pistol butt and that skinny wrangler weighing in with kicks whenever a clear shot presented itself.

The conductor never moved an inch, just set still like a wooden Indian in front of a cigar store. He was scared of Jules himself; too scared to go to the aid of his friend. The mules spooked when the club whacked again and Frank give another call for help. The coach lurched forwards and the conductor fell off into the middle of the fight whether he wanted to or no.

That team was sure enough off to the races. They kept to the road for fifty yards or so, and then the right rear wheel hit a rock or something and we went bowling off across the desert.

I vaulted into the driver's box and took up them ribbons like I was born to it. I figured that team would be right sassy when they sensed an untried hand at the reins, and right I was. For the first minute of sawing back and forth, they paid me no mind at all.

Up ahead, a bright patch of moonlight was sliced in half by a long, black line. That could only mean one thing: a dry wash or arroyo lay ahead, with us heading straight for kingdom come.

But I had already found out what I needed to know. No matter how well matched a pair of mules, one will always exert hisself a little more, be a little stronger. And of the two leaders, it was the righthand critter.

So, I hooked up a double handful of reins and cranked the leaders to the right, knowing I could use the natural ability of the stronger mule to pull the coach around in a circle. And wheel about we did, with the rear of the coach sliding over shaley rock and spurting up gravel, and me having no time to pay any attention to any boulders smaller than the size of my head. We did bounce some, right enough.

We did not really come close to flying over the edge of that canyon, but we whipped by near enough for me to spit into it, and that ain't no lie. We come flying up on the scene of the battle again. I heard the blast of a six-gun and I knowed things was serious. I steered that team right into the thick of the fight, just missing where the conductor had landed on his head. We scattered folks to both sides, and when the shoulder of the righthand leader mule knocked Jules down, the pistol went flying out of his hand. Then I give a whoa, and them mules stopped as sweet as if they had knowed me forever.

Maybe it was the two against one, or the blindside nature of the attack . . . or maybe it was the scared, higher squeak to Frank's voice that come out when he yelled for help that made me do what I done. I pitched off of that coach, right on top of Jules just as he was getting to his feet. It was like dropping a watermelon on somebody's head, catching him sudden and knocking him down again.

The other fella scrabbled in the dust, looking for that gun, and Frank give him a good right to the chin. Then Jules closed with me and punched me in the gut. He let me know I was going to live to regret interfering, if ever I lived so long. I was already enlisted for the whole of the war, too late to reconsider, so I folded my fists together like I was swinging a bat and uncorked a two-handed swing that Jules walked straight into.

The blow knocked him down on one knee, but he come up again with a flurry of punches and all I could do for a time was protect myself. I slipped in jabs that cut his lip and pasted his eye. He hollered for the other fella to throw him the gun. Things looked bad.

Frank and the other bushwhacker rolled over on the ground, and it scared me when I seen Jules's partner come up with the revolver. He swung it round to draw down on Frank, but Frank knocked the gun aside just as the trigger got pulled.

There was another blast and a spurt of flame that most blinded me, then Jules give a grunt of pain and stopped swinging. A second later, he keeled over, a dead man, from being shot in the back by his pard.

When the skinny fella seen what had happened, he throwed the gun down and took to his heels and we never saw him no more.

Now about this point, another gunshot come from inside the coach. It didn't hit nobody, thank the Lord. I ducked down anyways, and when I peeked up I seen just a hand holding a tiny .25-caliber pistol and waving it out the window. Seems Sam and Orion, being the only two passengers in the coach, had undid the curtain flaps just enough to poke the gun through, but not enough to aim.

"Put that thing away, 'fore you hurt somebody," I yelled. The pistol disappeared like it was sucked back inside, and then I heard Sam's voice real quaky like. "Jim? You out there? Is it Injuns?" I told him everything was alright now, but to stay inside and not to shoot no more.

The conductor was coming around, so I loaded him into the coach and told Sam and Orion to tend him, whilst I went and checked on Frank. I was afraid to go into the station, on account of not knowing if Jules had any more accomplices lurking about.

Frank was breathing real hard and ragged, hunched over, with a hand pressed to his side. About the time I got to him, he give a lurch and held out his hand to me for support, and even though the moonlight made it look black, I knowed that hand was covered with blood. He passed out then, and throwing him over my shoulder, I made for the hovel that passed for a station, danger or no.

Once inside, I swept some dirty tin plates onto the floor and laid Frank down on the rough plank table. I got a lantern lit and a basin of water laid by, then I turned to Frank. With my jackknife I slit Frank's shirt up the side to examine the wound.

I found the wound, right enough. The first shot had ripped through Frank's flesh, between rib and hipbone, just above that broad belt. It was not a deep wound, more of a furrow than a hole, but it had bled considerable. It was a wonder Frank could have done all the fighting he did, with that gouge bleeding all the while.

But the other wonder was what else I found. Frank was a woman! That wide leather belt and blousy shirt had concealed it, but without the disguise, there weren't no mistake.

I went on washing and bandaging the wound, and when I was most done, Frank (and I don't know no other name to use) come around. First thing she said was, "You know, don't you?"

I nodded.

Then she said, "Does anyone else?"

I said, "No, ma'am. I reckon not."

Right then and there she made me promise not to let on to nobody never. She didn't even ask me how bad she was hurt or what happened to the others until after I swore to keep her secret.

I drove the team on to the next change of drivers where we said good-bye. "Never mind what you hear folks say about the Injuns," Frank offered by way of advice. "They're mostly peaceable. Bushwhackers like Jules will try to get them blamed or at least rile things up. Watch out for the others of his kind."

Chapter 7

The last stage stop before we reached Carson City was just outside Fort Churchill, about twenty-five miles east of our destination. The fort—not a real stockade, just a dozen buildings built of adobe bricks—stood in a bend of the Carson River. The fort got its start a year earlier than my arrival in Nevada Territory, in the summer of '60. The Paiute Indians, also called the Washoe tribe, had gone on the warpath and killed some folks at a place called Williams Trading Post. What followed the massacre was something called the Paiute War or the Battle of Pyramid Lake.

The killings had started when some white men stole a couple Indian girls. First the Indians whipped up on the whites, and then the whites hollered for help from the U.S. Army in California and they scared the Washoes into clearing out.

But the miners and other folks of the Washoe mining region wasn't certain that the Indians wouldn't try again. They got the army to set up Fort Churchill, so as to keep some defenders nearby.

Things was not entirely calm yet, what with the war just being a year old and feelings pretty sore on both sides.

There was two companies of Yankee infantry and one of Yankee dragoons at the fort. The dried mud block barracks was nought but half done; the other half still building. But there was a couple hundred men plus weapons and ammunition stored there.

The stage depot hard by the fort was called Bucklands. The soldiers spent their spare coins there, friendly Indians traded, and miners coming to the Virginia City diggings passed through. Bucklands was on the Pony Express trail and the route of the new Overland Telegraph. All in all, a right busy place for a flat spot amongst the sand and sage.

We stopped at Bucklands only long enough to swap the teams. A big, swaggering, red-faced man, two-thirds drunk and louder than a brass band, hung onto the rail of Buckland's porch like it was a pulpit and held forth for the entire territory to hear. "Blast the Yankees and blast Abe Lincoln and blast the abolitionists! All the South wanted was to go in peace, but oh no, old Abe wouldn't let 'em. Well, he'll regret it, mark my words, yessir! Long live the Confederacy! Long live Jeff Davis! Hurrah!"

Sam poked his head out of the coach window and asked the driver who that fella was, and weren't he scared to be so loud, what with all the Union soldiers so close and all?

"Pay him no mind," said the reinsman, "he's drunk. But stranger," he added in a real serious manner, "don't cross him, neither! That there is Bill Mayfield. Him and Ruff Hardy and Sam Brown, and them other secesh rebels, drunk or sober, they ain't scared of nothing. And they don't carry them pistols just for looks, neither."

Sam pulled his head back in then, but not before I heard him remark to Orion, "What was that you said to Redpath?

Out west where there aren't any dangerous rebels?" The driver touched up the team and off we spun, so I never did hear if Mister Orion made any reply.

———•••••———

We had the expectation that Carson City, being the capital of the territory and all, would be a sight more imposing than it was. Between Salt Lake City and Carson, there weren't anything big enough to be called a town, let alone a city, so I was ready for something that looked a mite civilized.

The stage swung up over the last rise that separated us from our intended home and dropped down into a sink. The road churned with alkali dust like it was steam boiling under the wheels. Due west was the peaks of the Sierras; a great big, spiky wall, eight, nine, ten thousand feet high, like God had to build a mighty big fence to keep the desert from overrunning the world.

The driver hollered over his shoulder to me, "There's Carson!" and he pointed with his whip.

I wiped the dust out of my eyes, best I was able, and I strained to see what he was pointing at. I made out some white specks at the bottom of them mountains. I thought I was looking at beehives, or chicken coops, so I hollered back, "Where you looking?"

And he said, "Right there!" and he pointed again.

Them beehive, chicken-coop-looking things was Carson City! The town was all built of whitewashed boards, and they was so puny compared with what God did out of granite, I just had to laugh.

We rattled into the center of town, and I do mean

rattled, because the dry air and alkali dust had leached all the moisture out of the wheels and the spokes was fairly fixing to give up and turn loose. Our coach shared the road with a pair of freight wagons, hauled by ten pair of mules each. That's how they moved fuel, food, furniture, and the other fixings of civilization over the mountains. Pulling up in the middle of the downtown block of buildings, the driver whoaed the mules. Our journey across half a continent come to a sudden end.

I climbed down off the roof of that coach for the last time and stepped onto a plank boardwalk. I helped the stationhands unload the bags out of the boot, and then I took a shot at shaking myself free of the dust.

That's when I noticed some fellas looking at me and pointing, and others laughing right out loud. I even turned around to see what was so funny, but there weren't anything to be seen. I said to Sam, "What's so all fired humorous? What is these folks laughing at?"

He looks me up and down and answers, "Jim, I expect they are watching you emerge from your alkali cocoon. You are, without a doubt, the whitest black man I, or any of them, have ever seen!"

Such was my arrival in the Nevada Territory.

Sam and Orion fetched up at a boardinghouse run by an Irish lady, joining fourteen other fellas what was already staying there, all in one big room. I couldn't stay inside the rooming house and no other place would have me neither.

Sam said that this was only temporary, 'til him and his brother got theirselves a place of their own. I could stay with them when they did, and in the meantime, they fixed me up a tent out behind Mrs. Flannigan's place. She said she'd feed me alright, if I would chop the sagebrush branches for the cook fire, wash the dishes, and such. Which is exactly what I did for two or three days.

Now there ain't nothing dishonorable about washing dishes for your keep, but it seemed to me that I didn't come west to work as no house slave. My aim was to catch enough money quick to get me another team and go to freighting again. What with flour selling for fifty dollars a barrel, people was paying jewelry prices to get stuff hauled in from San Francisco. But first I needed a bankroll. There was all kind of stories about folks striking it rich in the silver mines of Virginia City, and I made up my mind to ask Sam to stake me to some prospecting gear. He showed up outside my tent looking mighty down-in-the-mouth himself.

"What's the matter, Sam? You look like somebody done stole your joy."

"That's about the size of it, Jim," he said. "You remember when my brother said that he was authorized to have an assistant?" I nodded with the recollection. "Well, what my brother forgot to find out was how his assistant was supposed to get paid. Seems he overlooked the little detail that if he hired a helper, it would come out of his own one hundred fifty a month."

"That's bad, ain't it?"

"It is, since Orion is trying to save up enough money to get a house for his wife and daughter. I can't ask him to support me too. I'll have to think of something else. Matter of fact, I got an idea."

It was just about sundown, and what they call the

Washoe Zephyr was kicking up. That wind blows regular in the afternoon, ripping down the east side of the mountains and playing rough with shingles and loose boards and careless chickens. My tent flapped so bad that I could hardly hear, so I said to Sam that we ought to go round to the front of the boardinghouse and stand to the lee of the breeze.

When we found a quieter spot, Sam lit up his meerschaum pipe, so I commenced talking instead of him. "What about prospecting?" I said. "Why don't you and me team up and find us a silver mine?"

He raised them bushy eyebrows and studied the bowl of the pipe for a minute. "Thought of that," he said at last. "But from what I hear tell, everything in Virginia City has already been claimed six ways from Sunday. There are new diggings down south of here, but I don't know yet if it's for real."

It was my turn to look glum. I really counted on making a silver strike. "Guess I could hire on as a miner for someone else," I said. "Or maybe a driver or a cook."

About that time, a fella come sailing down Main Street like a little boat driven by a storm. His coattails blowed halfway up his back and he needed both hands to keep his hat squished down on his head. He was aiming for the boardinghouse, but he had to line himself up and come over on the slant a good deal upwind, otherwise he would have missed it.

He lit in the middle of Mrs. Flannigan's porch, near bowled over Sam and me, give a gruff "'Scuse me," and pushed on inside. But not before I seen his pointy, ratlike face.

"Quick!" I said to Sam. "Do you know who that fella is? And what he's doing here?"

"Met him at supper," Sam answered. "Name's Ward. He's a new roomer . . . fifteen of us in happy intimacy upstairs now—but he says he's just here a couple nights on business, then back to Virginia City. Why? Do you know him?"

I nodded. "His name is Ward alright! He was the slave boss what sold me and stole the money. Lowest man next to old Trueblood I ever met."

"Did he recognize you?"

"Doubt it. When he last seen me, I weren't but eleven or twelve."

"So? What's your worry? Even if he did remember you, what's he gonna do? Turn you in as a runaway and put his own neck in a noose?"

I shuddered like the wind was chill, only it wasn't. "I dunno what he might do. He has a real wicked feel about him. What's his business that he come here for?"

"He's a foreman up on the Comstock Lode. Some kind of boss for the Chollar Mine, I think he said."

That killed any thought I had in my head of going to work in a mine, if that was the kind of foremen they hired up Virginia City way. "What was your idea," I said, "the one you started to tell me about?"

"Oh," Sam remembered. "Governor Nye suggested it. They use a lot of squared-off timbers down in the mines, for bracing and so forth. Anyway, a man can stake a patch of pine trees up on the mountain, just like a mining claim. What do you think?"

"How far we got's to go?"

"Just due west. If you're game. We can go in about a week."

"Can't we leave tomorrow?"

———————◆◈◆———————

Waiting to get on with our timber claim, the nights was long and lonesome and the wind howled down from the mountains and made me feel restlesslike and all dissatisfied in my soul. When that dark feeling come upon me it seemed like there was some piece of myself that had gone missing and I just had to find it. Trouble was, I didn't know what *it* was or where I had mislaid *it*. That being the case, I did not know where to begin looking.

Orion and Sam had found us a place to live, a little two-room house, so I weren't out back in a tent no more. But that was all that happened worth remark.

About another week passed in boredom and unease, when my soul was stirred the afternoon the Washoe Zephyr come swooping down on Carson City again, carrying the scent of sage and pine and dust into the valley.

Carson were only four blocks of white, clapboard houses with the blue Sierra mountains rearing up in the west and all the wide desert stretching out to the east. One-story buildings bordered a town square on three sides. The fourth side was open to the desert. In the center of the square stood a sixty-foot-tall flagpole. In this space, teamsters parked their wagons whilst they went into the Ormsby House for a snort of whiskey to see them on their way.

On that afternoon the wind blowed so fierce that Old Glory stood straight out from the pole like the canvas were a slab of wood painted red, white, and blue. Such a wind could blast granite smooth and suffocate man and beast alike if they was to be caught out in it for long.

Carson was packed with wagons and teams of mules and horses whilst the mule skinners took shelter. Critters stood with heads drooping down, eyes closed, ears laid back, and butts to the grit and wind.

From the window of Orion's house I could see all this misery. The Zephyr moaned around the corner of the little building and my soul begun to stir and pace and groan inside of me. Then that voice come to me, telling me that something was out there just beyond my vision, behind the curtain of dust.

"This is like to last a while," Orion said to Sam and me. "There was supposed to be a wagon train headed our way from Fort Churchill. Let's hope they had the good sense to linger there."

Sam and Orion went into the kitchen whilst I stayed looking out at the dust storm. I could hear the two brothers talking about the war. The Union Army of the Potomac was taking a licking from the rebs and Jeb Stuart's cavalry in particular. The news weren't good.

From that dismal topic the two brothers took off talking about the silver strikes in the mountains away south and up Virginia City way, but none of it held my interest. Deep inside I was listening to another voice, but I could not understand the meaning of it.

I must have stood at that window for an hour or better. I seen two freight wagons roll in. The drivers, bent against the wind, faces covered with kerchiefs, tended their horses and then beat it into the hotel. I knowed that there wouldn't be a bed to be had in Carson City that night unless a man was willing to share with a half-dozen others. As for me, I would bunk right there in Orion's parlor on the floor and be grateful for it.

I heard Orion say, "A man can't know who to trust in these parts . . . The place is crawling with secesh . . . Captain Moore at Fort Churchill doesn't believe it, but I say we'll have the rebel army rising up here in our own backyard before the year is out."

"That only makes sense," Sam said. "The rebs can make as good use out of Nevada silver as the Union can."

So they talked on about Union spies and secret cells of rebels intent on capturing Nevada for their cause. I thought to myself that anyone crazy enough to want Nevada ought to take her and welcome. I was yearning for a long, cool look at the green Missouri countryside and a bath in Mississippi River water.

About that time I seen something just out beyond the brown curtain of swirling dust. First off I thought it looked something like a sail on a ship all billowed out in the gale. Then I figured it were a critter trying to make its way into the lee of a building across the square. There was a flash of red and I seen that I was looking at a woman's hoop skirt and petticoat, which had blowed up over her head. There was two legs, covered in ruffled bloomers, stumbling against the wind. The fabric of the skirt pushed her back one step for every two she took.

"Glory be!" I said out loud.

Sam hollered out at me, "What do you see?"

"A female woman just blowed into the square!"

She fell down on her back in that same instant and I was out the door and sprinting across the square and through the tangle of wagons and teams to her side.

She was making choking noises, sort of angry and scared and flustered all at the same time, as if she had fell into water and was trying to swim. Them hoops was all the way up and over her shoulders, and she was trapped just like as if she had a gunnysack tied over top of her. Them long legs was kicking against the wind, but it didn't do her no good.

So she commenced to hollering. "Halp! Somebody halp me!"

Sam come along just behind me. His voice was near drowned out in the wind. "What has blown in here, Jim?"

"A hoop skirt with a woman trapped inside," I said. Then I bent down and grasped the bottom hoop, which was at the top. I gave it a tug until I could see the crown of the female's head.

"Is she a keeper? Or do we throw her back?" Sam shouted.

In spite of the state of upheaval she was in at the time, I could see that beneath the coating of alkali dust she was young and beautiful and colored same as me. Later I found out that she was the child of a union between a runaway slave and a Cherokee Indian in the territories.

My soul rejoiced! All my life I had the feeling the wind was going to blow some good fortune my way, and here she were all in a heap, sitting at my feet.

She stuck out her hand. "Don't just stand there, you fool! Halp me up!"

I done as I was told, but I could not find any voice in

me to speak even one word to her. I stepped back out of her way as she pounded on her red dress until it become obedient and stayed where it ought.

"Folks call me Sam." Sam made as if to tip his hat, but it had blowed away.

"They call me Lark," she said, giving a little dip with her knees, "because I sing." I thought I had never seen a bird so beautiful.

I tried to tell her my name, but I just sort of croaked at her. She asked, "What ails him? Is he struck dumb?"

Sam answered. "Only smitten by the sight of unexpected beauty in such a place as this. His name is Jim."

I grinned and got sand in my teeth. She turned away from me before I could think of anything to say.

Sam knowed just what to say though. "Now, where have you come from, Madame? And tell us how you happen to arrive here on foot and in such a condition?" He bowed and offered her his arm to escort her back to Orion's house lest she be blown back the way she come.

"There is a wagon load of helpless women out there. We were bound for Virginia City to perform at the Virginia House."

I had heard tell of the Virginia House from a Union soldier on the porch at Ormsby's. The place was a hotel that served as a meeting place for the rebel sympathizers in Storey County. It had a new saloon and dance hall that was all ready and waiting for a troop of hurdy-gurdy girls to arrive from the South. So this gal was one of them. I knowed about such females. They was girls who danced with men for a dollar a dance. Some of them would do more with a man than just dance.

Sam looked Mizz Lark over real good. "Well, this ain't the Virginia House."

"Our wheel broke. They sent me on ahead to fetch aid."

A wagon load of females? Broke down in a dust storm outside of Carson City, Nevada?

This event were a sort of miracle to the teamsters gathered in the Corner Bar at the Ormsby House. In no time at all there was dozens of teams and wagons charging through the Washoe winds in search of fair ladies in distress. There was more wagons racing through the storm than there was ladies to rescue. As it turned out, there was one dozen stranded females and three dozen freight wagons and buckboards. In some cases, this led to violence among teamsters who had been good friends and companions for many years. Something like the Civil War, it was.

Whilst the rescue was being made, I had the good sense to stay put in Orion's parlor alone with Mizz Lark. She had lived most of her life in Louisiana and knew something about good food, so I whomped her up a quail egg omelette and fritters and at last I found my voice.

I told her all about myself and where I come from. I told her about my mama and Uncle Dimmy's inheritance and Sam and the riverboat and finally how I come to be here in Nevada.

"I'm a freeman, and I aim to stay free," I said. "I aim to make my fortune out here in the silver mines."

She smiled at me real sadlike, as if she knowed about dreams that sometimes come true but mostly do not.

"I hope you find everythin' you want." Then she looked down at her empty plate. "You sure do know how to take care of a gal."

I sat down across the table from her and took her hand. "I know I am making bold, Mizz Lark, but I got to tell you everything I been thinking." I nearly lost my voice again as all them sweet thoughts crowded up in my throat trying to get out all at once. "Well," I said, "you know when I seen this place I was wondering why I ever left the green fields of home. Then the wind blowed you into town and I says to myself, 'Jim, that there is the very reason why you come so far.'"

She pulled her hand away. "Please don't . . ."

She tried to put a stop to my declaration, but it were too late. I had started and now there weren't no halting me from telling all. I grabbed up her hand again.

"What I mean to say is this . . . I ain't never seen a woman so purty as you are. I ain't never heard any lark sing so sweet as when I first heard your voice."

"Please, Jim." She stood up and turned her back to me, then she went over and looked out the window. "You don't know nothin' 'bout me. 'Bout where I come from or what I am doin' here."

"I don't need to know no more than that I could love a gal like you."

"I ain't what you think. Ain't no sweet little lark."

"It don't matter to me." I went over to her and just stood close enough so as I could have touched her, but I did not. I knowed well enough what sort of life she come from and I did not want her to get the notion that I was like every other two-legged male critter who thought of her as something to be bought and pawed and wrestled around a dance floor.

She stared out at the dust blowing through Carson City. "I ain't free."

"Yes, you are," I said. "There ain't no slaves in Nevada. All that we left behind us. Every man and every woman gonna be free, no matter what color. Mister Lincoln is fighting over that right now."

"No. I ain't free to love a man. Can't sing for whoever I want." Her voice was soft and sad like someone telling of sweet dreams that couldn't ever come true.

I wanted to take her in my arms. Didn't she understand that nobody had a hold on her now that she had come west?

I told her this again. Told her I knowed women who had led a hard life who had been redeemed. I said that her soul was all that mattered to me and that we could make a new start; that I would treat her good and that she would learn to love me.

She give her head a shake, then put her hand on my cheek. "Jim." She said my name so tender that I knew her heart was listening to me. "I bought my own freedom."

"You see!"

"But listen . . . freedom had a high price. The boss of this troupe, Mister Ryeman, he bought me at auction. Put me to work in his place back in Natchez singin' and dancing as a hurdy-gurdy gal. You know what such things mean . . . When he heard tell of the war and the silver strike out here, he gimme a choice. A chance. Said if I wants to be free I can work my way to freedom. Seven years here in the West. Work off the price he paid for me and some more, then I can go where I wants to."

"That don't mean nothing!"

"I put my mark on his paper, Jim! Don't you see? That contrac' says I owes him all this money. Says I gots to work seven years or pay him five thousand dollars."

"Lark! Five thousand . . ."

"It was that or stay in Natchez with no hope of ever bein' free. One man the same as any other, I tole myself! Don't matter if I be in Natchez or Virginia City. Only here I figgered I could have some hope! Figgered I could cross off ever' day 'til seven years gets by. When some man paid his dollar for me to dance I figgered I close my eyes and think there would come a day . . ." She begun to cry soft and sorry like a youngin who done wrong and was shamed of it. "But now here you come along . . . big and strong and sayin' you could love me! An' I'm thinkin' mebbe I could love you too. I didn't s'pect it, Jim! Not so soon! Not b'fore I even start . . ."

I put my arms round her and she leaned against me. Her tears made my vest damp. I just let her cry too. I was remembering them girls on down at Madame Nellie's in New Orleans when I was just a youngin. Sometimes they would come out to the cookhouse and just cry whilst my mama would hold them like they was children. By and by their broken hearts would find comfort to face whatever they must. So I held Lark in my arms just like Mama would.

Then I remembered how Uncle Dimmy said most folks was slaves of one kind or another. Didn't matter what color they was, most folks was owned by something and needed to be set free.

The old man's voice spoke clear to my heart as if he was sitting right there in his willow rocker. "Glory be, chile, listen up! Listen t' Uncle Dimmy now! You knows it only be love dat cut dem chains loose, Jim! Ain't nothin' but love kin set a soul free! Does y' love dis gal?"

He was telling me something! Like always, he was saying that there were some way to open that cage and let Lark fly free! I couldn't see the way clear yet, but it were there waiting for me!

"What you tellin' me, Uncle Dimmy?" I whispered.

Then Lark, she looked up at me. "What you sayin', Jim?"

I looked her square in the eyes. "I'm sayin' I loves you, gal, and I'll get you free!" I blurted this out though I did not know how I would do this.

"If you try to steal me away from Ryeman he'll shoot you dead! I seen him do it to a white man who tried to take away one of the girls from the house in Natchez. The law said Ryeman was right. No, Jim! That man would just hunt us down. Kill you and take me back . . . Seven years and then I be free. Ain't no man wait so long as that. Not when a gal sells her soul to buy freedom. Not when my contrac' is owned by a man like Ryeman."

"I'll get the money."

"How you gonna do that?"

"I loves you gal. I come all this way just to find you and love you. Such things don't happen by accident! I'm gonna find some way, that's all."

I had made up my mind by the time the women come back to Carson. We watched them through the window. In the lead wagon there was a coarse woman with dyed red hair and her face paint all smeared on her face from the wind.

I made as if to hold Lark from going, but she pushed me away and dried her eyes.

"I can't let you go," I said in misery.

"Stay here, Jim!" she told me. "They can't ever know I met you! You hear me? You're a black man! Ryeman will shoot you dead if he just 'spects you have an eye out for setting me free!"

I held onto her hand. No man was ever so filled up with the miseries as I were. "I'll follow you!"

"No!" she shouted. "Stay away from Virginia City! Can't you see how it would kill me to know you was so near? To know that you was watching other men come and go into that saloon and that I was there . . . If you loves me, stay away from me! Clean away, you hear? You gonna break my heart with hope that can't come true!"

I let her leave me then. I watched her walk back to that life because I knowed what she was saying was the truth. First I had to make the way to set her free. Five thousand dollars! I would make my fortune and come find her and pay the price and take her with me!

Chapter 8

Early the next morning Sam and me gathered up rucksacks filled with one change of clothes each, canteens, axes, bacon, cornmeal, beans, coffee, sugar, and salt. We rolled up the canvas that had been my tent and lit out for the mountains and the timber claim that was going to be the start of our fortunes.

The lake we was headed for was named Lake Bigler, after some California politician. But there was already a move afoot to change its name on account of Bigler not only had rebel leanings, he was a crook to boot. Most folks around Washoe area called it by its Indian name anyhow: Tahoe.

In Paiute, Tahoe means "Big Water" or "Sky Water." Either handle fits it right well. Sam said Tahoe means "Grasshopper Soup," because the Indians had named it after the meal they liked best in the whole world; but he was joshing and just made that up.

Anyway, Lake Tahoe, or Lake Bigler, was only ten miles or less away, but it was most nearly straight up a mile of mountain! We figured to be a day just hiking there and setting up camp.

The first half of the trip was up a narrow, rocky gorge, full of boulders and sagebrush. It was so still and hot in that canyon that I would have been grateful for a Washoe Zephyr to come by, but it seemed even they didn't have no truck with that place. It looked and felt like a hunk of desert, only tipped up on edge.

We got to the head of the canyon, finally above the chaparral and into the start of a pine forest. Sam allowed we should stop and rest; seemed he was most wore out with guiding. I have to smile when I think of it, because I was carrying both axes and all the supplies. He was toting only his clothes, but I reckon the responsibility of being pilot just tuckered him out.

We sat down on a big rock where we could look out across the Carson Valley. We munched on some biscuits saved from dinner the night before and calculated how far we'd come and how far we still had to go. Sam looked around at the hillside of pine trees and said, "What's wrong with right here?"

"Ain't it claimed already?"

Sam fished around inside his shirt pocket and pulls out a map the governor had give him. He studied it a min te, and then he said, "No. All the claims are inside the bowl of the lake. These trees haven't been claimed yet. This is perfect! We don't have to climb any further at all."

"But I thought the idea was to cut timber so as to float it to the sawmill on the lake. What are we gonna do here? If'n we cuts logs on this hill, they'll sure enough roll clean back to Carson and no way to stop 'em."

"Don't you see?" Sam said, all excited. "That's the beauty of it. We claim this grove, or the whole hillside even!

Then we show some businessman down in Carson what a great opportunity it would be to have a sawmill right there. Think of all the transportation cost that would be saved! Somebody will come along to buy our claim in no time."

"Buy our claim? Ain't we gonna work it ourselves?"

Sam looked shocked. "No, no. We're prospectors, don't you see? We locate a great opportunity for someone else to buy off of us. First come the prospectors, then the investors, then the developers, then the laborers, and along in there somewhere are speculators. But see, we get paid before anyone!"

"So what does we have axes for?"

"Because we have to work the claim first to prove it's ours. Then we can sell it!"

I begun to understand why he had been so all fired eager to have me for a partner. "What kinda work?"

"Oh nothing much!" He waved his arms like a scrawny white bird not quite making it off the ground, which was his way of letting me know that the amount of work required was most next to nothing.

"Uh-huh," I said. "Like what exactly?"

"We have to mark the boundaries, put up a dwelling, and show that we have begun to log it . . . that's all."

"Uh-huh."

"Really, Jim! We can start right now. Let me have one of the axes. I'll do the hard part, lopping off limbs all around our claim to mark it, while all you have to do is start felling trees to build a cabin."

"Whatever you says, Mister Sam. But say, is you sure these is the right kind of trees? They look pretty small." I pointed behind me on the ground to where a chipmunk run up and grabbed up a little pinecone. "'Sides, these here cones must have something in 'em worth eating." I busted another cone with a rock and picked out some seeds to chew.

When I offered a couple to Sam he weren't interested. "So some squirrels will have to go someplace else for dinner! Come on, let's get started."

I seen there weren't no arguing with him, so I took up my ax and found a likely looking tree close by the only flat spot there was on that hillside. I reckoned to drop the first trunk right where I planned the door of the cabin to be.

I made the first cut on the side for the tree to fall, about halfway through. Then I changed sides and made the second cut above the first.

Sparing a glance back up the hill, I seen Sam "marking our claim." He would go up to a tree, chop off the tiniest limb he could find, then step back to admire the effect.

I went back to work, shaking my head, and with a flurry of chops I got through the trunk and the tree leaned. It give a big groan and the fall speeded up. Next there was a big cracking noise and a great crashing as the pine smacked into the ground, busting off all the branches on that side, but landing right where I planned. The thud of the tree and the noise made by the shattering limbs bounced away down the canyon in the still air.

When the echoes of the crash died away, there was still a high-pitched howl that I could not for the life of me place. Then the sound of rocks spattering underfoot reached me, and the howl turned into Sam yelling for help!

I thought it must be a snake. Couldn't figure what else there might be to be afeard of out there on that hill. When

I spun around, Sam was slipping and sliding back down toward me. Ranged across the hillside a hundred yards or so higher was a line of Indians, half a dozen, men and women. I seen a couple rifles in the group and the biggest man, him who come down first like their leader, had a hatchet in his hand.

He wore floppy leather pants with a sash around his middle and a buckskin shirt decorated with beads and crow feathers on the shoulders. His hair, dark and straight, just touched his shoulders, and framed a broad, stony face. His eyes was watchful though. I seen him look us over, checking that we had no guns and that there was only two of us. If their aim was to jump us, I meant to give a good account of myself with my ax before getting whupped, but first I aimed to try talk.

Sam skidded to a stop more or less behind me. I held up my hand, palm out like I seen traders do with Indians at stage stops. "We come in peace," I said.

"So do we," said the Indian in better speech than me. "My name is Numaga, but a lot of folks call me Little Winnemucca since my father is Chief Winnemucca. What are you planning to do with that piñon tree?"

It was right interesting how fast Sam got all his courage back. He hopped right out in front and introduced hisself. "This is our timber claim," he said. "For the mines."

"I thought so," said Numaga. "I saw your boundary marks." One of the squaws giggled at that. "You know, these trees are too small and the wood is too full of sap for good lumber. I think you need to go up by the lakeshore." Sam bristled up like he was gonna argue when Numaga went on. "Show you something too," he said, and he whipped that hatchet toward the nearest tree. Sam jumped back about a yard, but all Numaga did was knock down a couple pinecones and bust them open. "See," he said. "These are nut pines. My people gather the seeds to grind for flour. That's what we came here for."

I seen then that the womenfolk all carried woven straw baskets. Fact is, the men was already sitting down, having a smoke, and two of the women had already begun to gather cones and shake out the seeds.

Sam looked a touch embarrassed, but he never was much good at admitting a mistake. "I'll scout up ahead," he said, real abrupt and huffylike, and he took off up the trail toward the lake.

Numaga helped me gather up our tools, and before I set out after Sam I shook his hand. The name Winnemucca was familiar to me. The elder of that name was chief of the tribe whose menfolk had taken the warpath against the whites just a year earlier. And this was his son!

I kept the connection to myself. There was always some things it was better for Sam not to know.

＊＊＊＊

Sam moved out some faster after the meeting with the Indians, and it was not because the trail was easier nor the mountain less steep. We arrived at the summit overlooking Lake Tahoe in just two more hours.

In spite of the teasing Sam done later about its name, I knowed he was just as thunderstruck with the beauty of the scene as I was. It was a picture of the prettiest lake ever, and big: twelve miles across and twenty-five longways. It was ringed with forests of pine trees and cedars and firs, each a hundred feet tall or more, and circled with mountain peaks that jumped up from its very edge three thousand feet, some still capped with snow. And all them pinnacles and trees and snow reflected in a perfect mirror, so it was all doubled and I could hardly tell up from down.

I still ain't even begun to explain what Lake Tahoe looks like. I haven't even said a word yet about how many different colors of blue they is in the water, from pale blue-green at the edge to the very darkest blue-black out in the middle. And critters? Deer raised up from the meadow where they was grazing to look us over, then went right back to feeding. Squirrels and raccoons in the trees and beaver in the streams. Black bears and cinnamon bears, and birds of so many colors they was like a feathered flower garden.

All this we seen not ten minutes walk down from the summit, before we ever even come to the shore. Sam said it was "the noblest sheet of water on the planet," or like that.

I don't know what makes water "noble," but I say this: The bowl of Tahoe is one of God's private places to rest Hisself and admire what He done. When He gets tired of messing about with people, He just goes right on up there and sets down awhile to ease His mind.

Sam checked the map again and waved his hand toward the northwest and said, "This way." I didn't know if he was right or not, but truth to tell, it didn't matter to me none; ever which way was pretty.

We followed a stream downwards through a canyon. That creek was lined both sides with aspen trees, their leaves already turned as yellow as the sun, and fluttering in the thin breeze.

We reached lakeshore at the place where the stream

emptied into a rocky little cove. Right by the mouth of the creek was a rowboat. It was made out of planks, and its nose and tail was squared off 'til it weren't much to look at, but the oars was there and the seams was tight. Sam said we had come to the right place, since some of Governor Nye's boys had left the skiff there on purpose and it was for us to use.

The shoreline circled on northeast a ways before turning west, and since the place we was headed for was due northwest from where we stood, rowing across instead of walking around made perfect sense.

We loaded our gear, then Sam and I both stood looking at the oars and, for a time, neither of us spoke. Then Sam, he pulled out the map again, and I caught his drift. "I know," I said, setting down backwards and grabbing them paddles. "You has to navigate."

So off we went, me leaning my back into each stroke and Sam busting hisself to navigate proper. We did not make much progress at first. The water of the lake was so clear that you could see the bottom down fifty or a hundred feet, same as if it was ten. I pulled a half dozen strokes and Sam hollered out, "Look at that!" That naturally put me off my rhythm whilst I whoaed up to take a look.

Sometimes it'd be a rock big as a church that'd slide by beneath, same as if we was a bird flying over top of it. Other yells would mean that he had spotted another one of them monster trout schools. One time we counted over eighty before we realized we was only counting the topmost layer and there was more under those. We give up counting then and begun to wish to arrive at camp. Sam let on that there was a cache of some supplies, fry pan and so forth, that included a fish pole and some hooks. Every time we seen more fish and then remembered the fish pole it did speed us up again some.

Long about halfway over, the bottom dropped away off into the deeps. We couldn't see nothing down there no more, just darkest blue, the color of ink. There's something mighty disquieting about knowing that when you *could* see bottom it was farther than a church steeple is tall; so when you cain't see bottom no more . . .

Long about that time, Sam looked up from studying his map again and he said, "What's that?" and pointed ahead of us.

I fetched around in the thwart and at first I didn't see nothing to remark; just the same line of trees and one bare patch of rock we had been aiming for most of an hour already. Then I noticed a line of blue water a darker color than the rest of the surface; not so pale, more like the deep parts.

"What is that?" I said, not mocking Sam's words, but in real puzzlement. I stopped rowing again and we studied on it some. Either that line was getting bigger, fatter some way, or else it was getting closer.

Sam said, "You know, back in my steamboat piloting days, if the river water up ahead changed color, I knew it meant a sandbar or a shoal. But that was always a change that was lighter in color, not darker. Besides, there can't be a sandbar clear out in the middle here; it's too deep."

"Sam," I said as I kept on watching, "I can't see the rocks as close down to the waterline as I could before. That line must be a wave, coming right towards us."

Sam and me looked at each other, and then I commenced

to rowing hard, giving it all I had. Navigating was plumb forgot. We just aimed ourselves at the closest piece of land we could see and got after it.

We had not covered another quarter mile before that wave was upon us. The good news was the first wave that come did not amount to nothing over a foot high. But behind him marched rank on rank of his bigger and bigger brothers!

That skiff begun to slip and slide and roll and bob and I seen that we were right quick gonna ship more water than it could handle. "Sam," I yelled, "gotta turn back into the wind or she'll swamp!"

He just bit his lip and hung on to both sides. Spray blew off the tops of the waves by then and what had been smooth water was now all foamy. White crests, what the Indians call white horses, raced by on both sides, except for the ones that slapped us square on the bow and soaked me through in no time. "Bail!" I yelled to Sam, and he snatched off his hat and scooped up water to toss out.

Quick as he flung out a hatful, the wind throwed it back again, and more besides. I strained into the teeth of the blow, and made precious little progress. So little headway in fact, that I did not want to sneak a look at the shore, because once I did and it was so discouraging that I felt like giving up entire.

Instead of looking over my shoulder, I looked up. How bright and cheerful the sky was! It weren't black, nor threatening. What few clouds there was raced by like to say "'Scuse me, but I can't stay floating around here. I gots to be in Missouri by morning." It was awful, because it didn't look like an evil day at all, to be so scary!

I said, right out loud, "Lord Jesus, don't let me die on such a purty day as this!"

Now I was digging into every wave something fierce, clawing my way across the tops. Most every stroke pulled us down a roller, then we was pushed up the next whilst I recovered, and then I done it over again. I reached back for another pull, dug in with the oars, and most nearly shot myself right out of the boat!

Sam's mouth was open and I was mighty amazed myself. Just at that second, we arrived at a span of flat water, just like there was no wind at all. Sam, he allowed as how the currents of air were blocked by one of them tall peaks and sheltered us, just like cupping your hand around a candle flame to keep it from getting blown out.

He was mostly right, only it weren't just the mountains that was cupped around us that day, no sir. Along about fifteen minutes later, we pulled into the prettiest little harbor you ever seen, exactly what we had aimed for. It was stunning how calm it was there, if such a thing can be. If we hadn't wrung two buckets of water out of our things and built a fire to dry them, we might not have believed how much danger we had just come through.

———•◦•———

We did no boundary marking that night, nor did we cut any timber, save what we chopped up to keep our fire going. Autumn it might still have been on the calendar, but at six thousand feet, when the wind shifts around and blows off the lake straight into camp, you feel like the Sierra might just decide to go right to winter.

Next morning, I discovered that Sam had not only

wound hisself up in all the canvas we had for bedroll, but he had curled around the fire so as to keep it all to hisself. When gray light come along about five o'clock, I woke him up and pointed this out. He looked at the few remaining coals of the campfire and said I should stir around quick and put some more wood on before it went out entire. Then he pulled his head back in and went back to sleep.

I rustled up enough wood to get the blaze going again, which made me not only plenty warm but also wide awake. By then Sam was getting overheated, so he wriggled out far enough to tell me it was my turn to fix breakfast, then he scooched back a bit and told me to wake him again when the coffee was ready!

I took the coffeepot from the cache of stores and filled it and toted it back to the fire. I wanted so bad to dump that jug of icy lake water over my partner's head, but I resisted, somehow, throwed a double handful of coffee in, and put the kettle on to boil.

By the time the coffee was bubbling, I had bacon sliced and frying. The trotline set the night before had a big fish on it, and right soon he changed his skin for some nice cornmeal and was smoking in the pan too.

Sam told me that in order to show we done the work required to "prove" our claim, we had to build us a dwelling. He allowed that a nice log cabin with a rock fireplace would be very pleasant and could be used as a hunting and fishing lodge after we sold our claim for a tremendous sum of money.

I let him know that he weren't going to do no boundary marking then, if he wanted a cabin built. He was going to have to pitch in and help.

"Sam," I said, "there's a right straight sugar pine there that'd make a fine start. Whyn't you go on over and fell him?"

"What about you?"

"I'll be along after I clean up the dishes. You just get us started."

"I'll do that," he said and he shouldered an ax. He studied that tree that was maybe two feet through the middle and he give a swing that stuck the ax in the trunk to where he could not horse it out. Three or four inches and he finally wrestled it loose.

"Sam, less'n you plan to drop that tree into them rocks where we cain't do nothing with it, you'd best move around some," I said.

He give me one of them "I knew that already" looks and then he circled on around. I swear he looked most like a fighter sizing up the other fella in the ring. He give a little chop that wouldn't hardly have busted an egg, then he stopped and reared back on his haunches to look the situation over. "When did you say you were coming?" he asked me.

"Quick as I get ever'thing cleaned up. You just go 'long about business," I said. "Don't worry about me."

He was most teased enough, so I finished up the cooking gear and took after a tree myself. I found a likely stand of ponderosa pines and got to work.

When I got the first one ready to drop, I glanced over at Sam and give a yell. He had a right nice pile of shavings where he was standing, but he weren't very close to cutting through. He stood and watched my tree fall, then he dusts off his hands like he's really ready for work and goes back to swinging.

I dropped the second and the third, and then I heard him yell, "She's gonna go!" Sure enough, that sugar pine come flopping down. Course, it landed spraddle of our campfire and flung the frypan most twenty yards through the air, but I told him he done good anyhow.

Sam looked right proud of hisself. "Now, how do we go about piling these up to make our cabin?"

I scratched my chin for a minute and calculated on it. "Well," I said, "we got enough here for half of one wall, I reckon, after we trim all the branches off and cut 'em to length."

Getting a real narrow look to his eyes, Sam frowned and said, "You know, building a whole cabin just to prove the claim isn't necessary. Not at all. Why, we could build a lean-to and cover it with a brush roof and that would answer the needs of the law."

So that is what we done. By that afternoon we had a two-sided affair of poles and cedar boughs. The backside was a big rock and the front was left open toward where we planned the fire to be. We covered the top with more cedar branches and there we were. Sam said it was good enough and would serve no longer than we needed it before we sold the claim. Then he said we had to stop working for the day and go catch more fish for supper.

❖•❖•❖

By sundown our second night at the lake, we not only had a skillet of trout frying but a kettle of beans simmering and a pan of cornbread baked. I could not see that we had made an awful lot of progress toward being rich, but I also could not see how any rich man on the face of the earth could be any more comfortable than we.

Sam insisted that we build the fire up big and blazing after the cooking got done. He said he was cold, which is likely enough, but fact is, he was scared of bears. Whatever the real cause, our campfire was a beacon that could probably be seen clean across the lake, some twenty miles away. Most anybody could've steered by our camp that night.

And that is exactly what happened. Half the cornbread, half the beans, and all the fish had been ate up. Sam was laying stretched out by the fire, smoking his big bowled pale yellow pipe. He was spinning yarn after yarn about what he would do with the money from the timber claim.

First it was a trip around the world, then it was a home in San Francisco to start and afterward a sea voyage. Next he allowed how he could invest in the stock of up-and-coming silver mines and get so wealthy he'd have all them things and never work a lick in his life.

I contented myself just letting him spin. It didn't cost nothing to dream thataway, and where's the harm? His ramblings didn't call for no response from me, so I was left free to dream about Lark.

Anyway, he went on to have a debate with hisself about whether he'd build his home out of stone or brick, and midway through the discussion he took off his little round spectacles and give them a wipe with his shirttail.

The debate come to a sudden halt and I seen him peering out into the dark of the hillside. When he recollected that he didn't have his glasses on, he screwed them up to his face and squinted again.

I had heard strangers coming for about ten minutes before Sam took notice. It didn't worry me none, since we didn't have nothing worth stealing. Besides, anybody who wanted to sneak up on the camp would not have allowed theirselves to make noise. I heard a dog yapping and the soft tread of several pairs of feet. Mind you, they weren't noisy in the white man sense of the word; they just wasn't trying to be extra quiet.

Sam slithered into the lean-to and caught hold of his pistol. "Jim," he said, "there's somebody creeping up on us!"

"Put that away before somebody—mostly likely me—gets hurt," I said. "It's just somebody that seen our fire—prob'ly seen it from Salt Lake City." About that time we heard Numaga's voice halloa the camp. "Come on in," I yelled back.

Presently a file of Indians appeared out of the dark. Numaga and his wife, whose Washoe name I forget, but it meant Twilight, had their son with them. The boy was only five or six and he had a puppy yapping at his heels. The fourth Indian was another brave we had saw the day before; his name was Echapa—Coyote.

"Come and set," I offered, "an' help yourself to the beans and cornbread. We've already eat our fill." Sam laid his pistol on the ground, but he kept his hand near it and his eyes stayed fixed on the hatchets belonging to the Indians.

"We are on our way home," Numaga said, gesturing at a cone-shaped straw basket that Twilight carried on her back with the aid of a strap across her forehead. "We saw your light."

Twilight pulled bowls out of a sack slung at her waist and commenced dishing up the beans. She fed Numaga and

Echapa first, then the boy, and last of all, took some for herself. They used pieces of cornbread to sop up the juice and scoop the beans into their mouths. Even if I couldn't understand what they was saying, they seemed to be enjoying my cooking.

Presently Numaga give a belch and patted his belly. "You are a good cook," he said. "Sometime you must come to our village and Twilight will feed you."

Numaga and me talked quiet about the silver strikes and the new flood of white folks coming to Washoe and about the war back in the States. He was a right well-informed man, anxious to see his people survive against what he judged was superior numbers and force.

Sam called the boy, named Togoa, over to him. Though the child, whose name means Rattlesnake, understood little of what Sam was saying, he still looked up wide-eyed at the paleface with the curly brown hair.

Sam explained to his audience how he'd chopped down all the trees and built the lean-to and caught all the fish in the lake. This took awhile before he finally gestured toward the one true accomplishment of his: cutting down the sugar pine.

Togoa's mama looked at where that sugar pine lay across the old campfire pit and she said something to the boy in their own tongue. Right away Togoa jumped up from beside of Sam, and run over to the tree. "Washoes like the sap from sugar pines," Numaga explained to me. "Fire makes crystals that are good to eat."

Sam looked sour at losing his listeners so abrupt, because Twilight and Echapa left off listening and went after the pine syrup too. Sam shrugged his shoulders and got up to watch as the youngin picked up a rock to bust the sugar crystals off the tree trunk.

All at once the boy give a scream and throwed the rock down. Then he run to his mama and hid his face in her skirt.

Sam scrambled to where the pistol was laying, certain that the Indians had showed their true colors at last and we was about to be scalped. When he was most nearly there, he tripped over a rock, stumbled, lost his glasses and kicked the campfire apart. A boot-toe of embers rolled straight into our lean-to, but nobody paid no attention right then.

Echapa also run back and he grabbed up a burning stick from the fire. He said something to Numaga whilst I grabbed Sam by the arms and shook my head, telling him to hold on a bit. The scrawny pup run around in circles, yipping and getting underfoot.

Whilst we watched, Echapa dashed back to the sugar pine and thrust his torch around on the ground like he was looking for something. He give a yell that I admit started the prickles up my neck, and he pounded the earth with that torch. Finally he stood up and called to Togoa something that must have been "It's all right now," because the boy looked around from hiding his eyes.

"Scorpion," Numaga explained. "Washoes think scorpions are the most wicked spirit creatures there is. Had to kill it quick or we would all have evil dreams tonight."

Now I don't know how wicked that particular insect was, but he sure was the bearer of bad news for us. Sam coughed and said, "Did you throw some green branches on the fire? Where's all this smoke coming from?"

The smoke was coming from them hot coals smoldering

in the cedar boughs of our shelter. Sam and me grabbed up two hatfuls of water from the lake to douse the fire, but it was too late before we got back.

When we were still twenty feet away, one side of our lean-to busted into a sheet of flame and roared up into the sky. Worse yet, hanging over the boulder that was the back wall was another big cedar with its branches drooping down.

Them flames licked that standing tree and must of liked the taste, because it eat straight up into the crown. Sam and me knowed there weren't nothing to be done, so we grabbed up our gear and went down to the waterline.

The evening wind off the lake blowed the flames into a nearby pine, and then another and another. Pretty soon pine cones was exploding like bombs and launching theirselves in all directions. And everywhere they hit, another fire sprung up.

It was powerful hot! We loaded all our belongings in the skiff and the Indians put their things in too. There weren't room enough for all the people, so we piled Togoa and the dog in on top and the rest of us held onto the sides of the boat and waded out waist deep in water.

The wind held so steady that the fire marched right up the canyon back of our camp and climbed the hill. We watched it chew up our timber claim just like a giant, glowing orange worm.

"I don't really mind," Sam said as we see the fire disappear behind one ridge, then start up the next one north like it ain't gonna stop before Canada. "I don't really care . . . having a timber claim is too much work. I just wish . . ." and he stopped.

"Wish what?" I asked.

"I wish the boy would quit yelling 'Whee!' every time another tree explodes," he said.

That were the end of our plans to be the Timber Barons of the Sierra Nevada. We didn't burn the entire mountain down, but only because about midnight, God took pity on such fools as we and sent over a thunderstorm.

That downpour only lasted an hour, but it took care of the fire. Trouble was, when we come out of the lake, all the dry timber near at hand was already burnt up, and what wasn't charred was soaked, same as we, so we spent the night huddled together with no way to either dry out or warm up.

Come morning, we headed out early on. The Indians had already left; departed without a sound or a good-bye, after the fashion of their kind.

I asked Sam if he wanted me to row us back across, but he said no. "Now that there is light enough to not fall off a cliff, I want to find some brush that didn't burn up so we can cook breakfast!" His boots made squishing noises when he walked and his hat flopped down over his ears like he'd been in the mountains a hundred years already. We left the skiff and trudged along the shore.

First little divide we crossed, we turned aside up a runnel where the fire had not gone and stopped for a mighty poor breakfast. The coffeepot got burnt up and the cornmeal, salt, and sugar was wet through and spoilt. I had salvaged the frypan and the bacon, and that was our meal. Sam had saved his pipe and his pistol in the ruckus, but had lost his glasses, so even dried out and warmed up, he were in a "don't cross me" mood.

When he proposed taking a shortcut over the mountain, instead of following the lakeshore back to the main trail, I give him his head. It started out well enough, with the stream's path climbing a gentle slope headed east, which agreed right enough with my own sense of direction.

Pretty soon though, the little creek come to a fork, with neither branch running true east. I favored one and Sam the other, and once more I let him pick.

Halfway up the slope the banks was steeper, rockier, and narrower, and we had to climb up out of there, or face a big backtrack later on. We scrambled straight up the mountain with no stream to follow and the hillside given over to low tangled shrub called manzanita.

There ain't scarcely a way to hold a line through brush that thick, especially when it gets taller than your head. Sam would never admit that the other way might be better. We wandered backwards and forwards on that slope, gaining a few yards, then giving it back to get by the next big thicket.

Eventually we did fight clean to the summit and come out on a bare rock ridge that looked back toward the lake on one side and out across Carson Valley on the other. Sam was right pleased, and he picked out the route for us to follow down.

I didn't see that any humans had ever come up or down that way, at least not in long years, but there was a deer trail and the east side of the mountain was more sparse of brush, which suited me. We come down the slope sliding in some places and eventually fetched up in a cottonwood-lined draw near the bottom.

By then I knew we was going to come out on the rocky divide just north of Carson City, so Sam didn't do so bad after all. We sat down in the shade of a cottonwood and rested a spell.

I leaned back against that tree trunk and pulled my hat down over my eyes. My thoughts was full of dish washing and such, or taking my chances with the mines and a foreman like Boss Ward. It come to me that there weren't no way to strike it rich and probably no white man would give me a job driving team, so my possibilities was limited. The urge to steal Lark and run away was powerful strong.

Brooding on this and that, I didn't pay much mind when Sam sat up and stared over the streambed toward a brushy thicket on the other side.

Real low, he said, "Jim. Jim. Wake up."

"What is it?"

"There's a bear in the trees. He's looking this way. I think he's seen us."

"So? Old bear ain't interested in us. You're too scrawny and I'm too tough."

"He is so! I see him staring straight at us. I'm gonna scare him off!"

And before I could stop him, out popped his peashooter and he loosed off three rounds.

"Quit that!" I said. But without his glasses, he was a better shot than with them on. He actually hit what he was aiming at. Except instead of a growl or such, the thing he was shooting went clang, clang, clang. "That ain't no bear," I said, "but I don't know what it is either. Just don't shoot no more, whilst I go see."

Under the trees, back in a hollow made by the overhang

of the cottonwood, was a humped-up shape that did sort of look bearish, at least to a man what needed glasses. There was a canvas covering over top of something, and it was plain from the place it was located that whoever put it there intended to leave it hid. By purest chance, we had sat down in the one spot it could be seen from.

It was a cannon.

When I stripped off the cover, there was a small bore weapon made to go into rough country, judging by the mount and the small size. It didn't look like no toy just because it was small. It looked plenty murderous all right. Something else: it looked new, meaning never used. The brass fittings was dulled but not overly so, and the wooden carriage and wheels was dried out, but not so as to spoil the thing for use. In short, it looked like whoever left it there was planning to come back and fetch it.

"Who would hide a cannon out here in the brush?" Sam wondered.

"You figger rebels? Or maybe somebody stole it from the army to sell to the Injuns?"

Either of them possibilities sounded bad. Whoever belonged to that killing machine would not like to find us nearby when they come after it. So we pushed along then, pretty sharp, aiming to bring up the matter to Governor Nye when we got back to town.

The fifth man in Orion's small parlor was not known to Sam or me. He come in with Governor Nye but stood quietly, shylike, near the door. "So, Sam," Nye boomed in his running-for-office voice, "you do not intend to pursue riches as a timber baron, eh?"

"No, Governor," Sam said. "What with the war and all, these are uncertain times. The bottom might drop out of the lumber market tomorrow, and then where would I be? Besides," he continued with a sly look my direction, "Jim is allergic to high altitudes. I don't see how we can pursue the claim."

Nye snorted, "I suspect you are the one who is allergic, but it's a reaction against hard work and not elevation!" Sam bristled, but when Orion and the governor burst out laughing, he begun to chuckle too. "There, that's better," Nye continued. "Don't take it serious, Sam. I have the same aversion myself. Why do you think I went into politics?"

"Governor!" Orion gulped with alarm. "Did you forget we have another guest?" He indicated the silent man.

"What? Oh, Willie won't quote that, will you? Sam, I'd like you and Jim to meet William Wright, better known as Dan DeQuille to the jackrabbits who read his column in the *Territorial Enterprise*."

The thin fella with the sparse sandy hair and scraggly pointed beard leaned against the door with an easy grin on his face. "I don't know, Governor," he retorted. "We scribblers can't pass up something newsworthy."

I seen mock alarm on Nye's broad features. "Won't any of my loyal constituents help me?" he pleaded. "Someone come up with a bone for this newshound to draw him off my scent."

"I've got one," Sam volunteered. "I have . . . Jim and I have discovered an interesting artifact."

"Really?" DeQuille said. "What might that be?"

"Jim and I have found a cannon, a mountain howitzer to be precise, that has been lost for close to twenty years."

"A cannon?" Nye rumbled. "Where? And how do you know so much about it?"

"Not so fast," Sam warned. "First, I want to know if the *Enterprise* will publish the story if I write it up. I published some letters back in Missouri."

"Certainly," DeQuille agreed. "If it's good we'll even pay you for it."

When the business doings was settled, Sam explained how he and I had located the cannon, leaving out the part about the imaginary bear. Then he said how he remembered something he read from Colonel John Charles Fremont's explorations back in the forties; how they had been dragging a cannon with them until forced to leave it behind because of the snow. "I checked Fremont's journal account and the description matches exactly."

"We'll go recover it," Governor Nye vowed. "We'll set it up in front of the state capitol . . . when Nevada is a state and we have a capitol," he added with a wink.

The *Territorial Enterprise* ran Sam's story. He signed it with the made-up name "Josh." Said that was what all the real correspondents done, not using their right names.

A few days later, Nye sent out a gang of his hangers-on to retrieve Fremont's cannon. They went right to the arroyo where Sam and I seen it, but the brassbound weapon was gone. They did find the canvas it had been wrapped in, lying in a heap, and the tracks where it had stood, but no trace of the cannon itself. Some folks said Sam planted the tarp and made the tracks hisself to give him something to write about, but Sam and me, we knowed different. But where it really got off to and who took it remained a mystery.

Chapter 9

Months went by without me making much progress toward setting Lark free. I done odd jobs and saved a little money, but it looked like a terrible long road. Then one day Sam tiptoed into the kitchen and motioned for me to follow him. He looked over his shoulder twice, like he was afraid somebody might be watching.

"Don't tell a soul," Sam whispered in a real dramatic tone. "Don't breathe this to anyone, but the word is *Aurora*."

Since there weren't nobody but the two of us in Orion's parlor, this seemed like extraordinary caution. "Alright," I agreed. "If'n you'll tell me what it means."

"It means our fortunes are made," he said. "Esmeralda mining district, little town called Aurora. Word just came today of a big strike there. If we head out tonight we can beat the rush and stake our claim."

I wasn't so sure. We had chased the timber claim and it had not amounted to nothing, but I was getting desperate. "It sounds good, Sam," I said, "but I needs work that pays regular. I reckon I needs a steady job 'stead of a claim."

He got around in front of me and looked me right in the eyes. "Jim," he said, "I wasn't gonna bring this up unless

I had to, but I can see you need more convincing. Do you remember the coach we came west in?"

"Course," I agreed. "I ain't likely to forget a contraption I rode on top of clean across the country."

"What was painted on the doors?"

With the sudden recollection come the meaning he was driving at. "A Spanish gal," I said, "and her name was . . ."

"Esmeralda," he finished with a triumphant sound. "It's a sign, don't you see? We are going to strike it rich in Esmeralda!"

Aurora was even less of a town than Carson City. Of all the buildings in the place, maybe half was actually boards and a handful was built of stone. The others was canvas tents over dirt floors, or heaped-up piles of brush, or misbegotten creations of stone and brush and boards all thrown together. And this was the biggest settlement in the mining district called Esmeralda.

There wasn't no main street neither. Fact is, there weren't no streets at all. Folks just plopped their dwellings down wherever they felt like it, mostly beside what stretch of ground they thought was most promising.

We set up our tent in a howling dust storm and I begun to have second thoughts about how good a sign that Spanish gal's name was.

Sam and me was huddled around a lantern pouring over a map of the place, when a voice hollered at us out of the storm, asking could he take shelter in our tent. The fella what come in dripping forty pounds of topsoil was an old prospector name of Billou. Dad Billou, everyone called him, because he seemed older than all the rest of the world. He had gray hair and a long gray beard. A short man, about shovel-handle tall, he walked kind of stooped over, but his disposition was cheerful. He had a choppy way of talking, as if he had only so much stock of words and didn't want to run out.

He'd been out to California in '49, made and lost a fortune in gold dust, been in the beginnings of the Comstock excitement and been shouldered aside by the bigger companies. Now he was known as a beans-and-flour man, meaning he made enough from the diggings to live from one day to the next, but just barely. But he claimed to have a nose that could smell silver ore, and Sam and me was in no position to overlook any offer of help. Still, when Dad asked if we knew what to look for, Sam naturally replied that we did.

The next morning we went off in three different directions to look for prospects. We was to meet up again at noon and compare what we found.

I tramped over five miles of hillside. I found lots of squirrel holes and rabbit holes and sage brush and weeds, but nothing like what Dad Billou had told me to search for.

Sam was already back at the tent. He was grinning ear to ear and couldn't wait to spill his news. "I told you Aurora would make our fortune!" he practically shouted. "Just look at this." He pulled the pockets of his jacket inside out and dumped a heap of rocks on the upside-down bucket that was our camp stool. "Look at the crystals sparkle in the light," he said. "And see that streak of color through this one? We've found it for sure!"

"Where did you find these?"

"That's just it! They came from the ravine in back of us. I hadn't walked more than fifty yards before I found them all!"

Along about then, Dad Billou got back. Sam saw him coming and held his finger up to his lips, meaning not to say a word. He wanted to just leave the ore samples out on the bucket and watch Dad's reaction.

Dad Billou come up to the tent flap and said howdy. "Seen nothin'," he said. "Followed a ledge. No good. Check far side later. That way." And with that he picked up the largest and shiniest of Sam's rocks and pitched it off toward the southeast.

"Wait!" Sam protested, snatching up the other stones out of harm's way. "What kind of a prospector are you? Smell silver ore, huh? You can't even see it when it's right under your nose!"

Billou apologized for throwing the sample away, then asked Sam what he wanted with a worthless piece of granite with a streak of feldspar. Only what he said was, "Granite. Feldspar. Ten cents an acre."

Sam looked a mite crestfallen, but I had not expected it to be all that easy, so I weren't so down as he. We decided that it might be smart for us to go together for a while, 'til we caught on to silver prospecting proper.

For the next couple months, we three tramped the hills, canyons, and ravines around Aurora. Sometimes Dad would pounce on a chunk of rock and Sam and me would hold our breath, but he always flung it down again.

Then one day we was just over the hill from the biggest strike that had yet been made in all Esmeralda. The mine was called the Wide West. The owners had dug a tunnel some two hundred feet into the hillside, following a ribbon of silver ore. They had been taking out several tons of rock a day and making only fair money. Then all of a sudden, while digging a new side tunnel or drift, they busted into a streak of pitch-black rock that crumbled to the touch. Dad said it was almost pure silver.

The ownership of the Wide West changed right sudden with its fortunes. Some fellas with secesh leanings, what they called Copperheads, moved in on the other owners. A .36-caliber suggestion was very persuasive, and the previous miners moved on somewheres else. The new headman of the Wide West was Bill Mayfield, the same loudmouth drunk we first seen at Bucklands station.

The reason that we come to the ridge in back of the Wide West was most mysterious to Sam and me. We had already prospected that knoll a half dozen times and not found anything. But Dad insisted that we go again.

We come to a place where a gully had washed slantways across the hill, exposing the rock layers beneath the soil. A dirty white streak of quartz showed at boot top height, and in that quartz stone was the thinnest black line you ever saw, almost like a thread.

Dad flung himself down on the ground next to the rock face and put his nose up against the quartz, just like a hound dog on a trail. "Dig here," he insisted. "Right here."

I swung the pick and busted the soil loose where Dad pointed his long, bony finger. Then Sam stepped in and shoveled it out 'til he come to solid rock again.

This kept up 'til I was standing in a hole about waist deep. Course, on Sam it was about chest deep. That time, when he took his place in the pit and flung up a shovelful of rock, the blade hit the shaft wall. It struck sparks and the debris flew only a foot or two in the air and right down Sam's neck. He threw down the tool, jumped up out of the hole, and went to shaking gravel out of his collar and the waist of his shirt. "That's far enough 'til you tell us what this is all about!" he said to Dad.

Dad agreed that it was far enough, and he jumped down in the pit hisself and went to sniffing the rock again. I could see that it was the fine, dark line that interested him, and that it had widened to toothpick width.

He called for a knife and I unfolded my Barlow and handed it to him. Dad scraped that black streak 'til he had a little pile of mineral in the palm of his hand, about so much as a dime would cover. Then he touched it to his tongue.

Sam and me watched Dad Billou climb up out of the hole, still staring down at his hand. "That's it," he said in his normal allowance of words.

"I told you we had covered this hill enough times," Sam said, taking Dad's meaning to be that we were through in that spot.

"No," Dad said, flicking the dust in his palm with a dirty fingernail. "Found the indication. Boys," he remarked with a twinkle in his eye, "this ore is the same as the new drift in the Wide West. It's a blind lead." Sam and I both looked at him in astonishment. It was the longest set of words strung together at once we had ever heard come from his mouth.

Mining law said that when a claim had been properly registered, the locators had the right to follow the vein wherever it led, down into the earth. But now and then, a second vein would run across the first at an angle; clearly a different streak of mineral entirely. If the second vein did not crop out on the surface it was called a blind lead, on account of no one would suspect that it was there.

The meaning of Dad's words finally sunk in to Sam and me. "You mean this is that real rich stuff they lately found in the Wide West?" I asked.

"And it's not part of their vein?" Sam continued.

"'Zactly," Dad agreed in his clipped speech. "Blind lead. Big rain the other night uncovered this top edge."

The miners working in the Wide West figured that they had just run into a rich body of ore on the vein they was following. But Dad was saying that this silver ore was from a different vein altogether and could be claimed by us as locators.

Sam and me danced around that four-foot-deep hole like we had plumb lost our minds. "We're rich!" Sam shouted. "Mansions and fancy carriages, here we come!"

Visions of a home with Lark flew around in my head. No mansion necessary, just her and me together.

Dad had a smile on his face when he said, "Celebrate later. Mark the claim now. Real work starts tomorrow!"

———————

The Monarch of the Mountains! I thought the name Sam give to our claim was a mite too grand. He said it was only fitting and proper, and that we would be glad we had not called it Sweet Sue, Root Hog or Die, or Tres Hombres, like other mines thereabouts. I put it to Dad Billou to decide. He scratched behind one ear and said, "Good enough," so that settled it.

Dad ground up a pea-sized lump of ore in his mortar and washed it out in his horn spoon. He got the faraway look in his eye that he had warned us meant he was "calculatin'." Sam and I stood by, silent and respectful 'til the computing was done. Presently Dad roused hisself and said, "Three hundred a ton, I'll be bound!" Anything over fifty dollars a ton in ore paid the costs of transport and milling, so this was a powerful rich strike indeed.

The rules of the mining district give us ten days to prove our claim. Like the timber business, this meant putting up a shelter, which we already had, and doing a reasonable amount of improvements. Dad said all that was needed was to turn the pit we dug into a proper shaft. He said that once we showed that the vein we was following was more than a surface pocket, then investors would jump at the chance to buy stock, what they called "feet," in our mine. He said that was how we would get the cash for the other necessities like a hoist, ore cars, and tracks.

Sam concluded that we was going to be nabobs of Nevada in no time. He wrote to the *Territorial Enterprise,* announcing the strike.

We knowed how Mayfield and his crew of Copperheads had moved in on the Wide West. Fact is, Sam had wrote another letter to the *Enterprise,* denouncing that whole crew for being sneaks, cheats, bullies, and thieves. He said the only reason his language was so mild was on account of a more accurate description would have scorched the paper. Even so, we figured they would be after the Monarch next. Sam and Dad and I organized ourselfs into a round-the-clock guard. Dad said if we could keep possession just long enough for the speculating to get rolling, we could hire all the guards we needed from then on. But for the next ten days, one man was to be always above-ground with a sawed-off twelve-gauge, even when the others was working within call.

On the morning of the third day, Sam was on guard and Dad and me had blasted our way down twenty-five feet. The vein turned, getting wider all the time, and we drilled the holes in preparation for starting an inclined tunnel. Over his right shoulder, Dad held the drill, a five-foot-tall bar of iron with a star-shaped point. I stood behind him, swinging the double jack, a ten-pound sledgehammer. Dad trusted me right well. After every strike, he'd rotate the drill a quarter turn so as to give the teeth a new bite, then I'd hammer away again.

We was about halfway done drilling our pattern of twenty-five holes to be packed with gunpowder and rock dust when the noise of a shotgun blast rumbled down to us.

My ears still ringing from the strike of the steel and the echoing boom, I kept the hammer in one hand as I swarmed up the notched planks. I come out of the shaft and seen Sam facing me, all alone. The coach gun was not in his hands. "What was that shot?" I said. "What's going on?"

Right then I felt a double circle of cold steel rings press into the back of my neck. "Only fired one," the boozy breath of Bill Mayfield informed me in a low tone. "Still got the other one for you, nigger, if you don't behave. Now drop that hammer and go stand by your nigger-loving friend."

I wondered if there was any way to alert Dad, but a shake of the double-barrel in my face warned me off and backed me up to stand by Sam. A half dozen of Mayfield's bunch, grinning at their success, flanked him to either side.

Dad Billou's head emerged from the pit, covered in rock dust and looking like an old, bearded gopher. "What's the ruckus?" he managed to get out before he was given similar treatment to Sam and me.

"Now boys," Mayfield said, "this here is part of the Wide West claim and we aim to work it. Can't have you trespassing, can we?"

Dad Billou sputtered into his beard. "Your claim? Side-winders! Skunks!"

"Now," Mayfield warned, "don't say nothing you'd regret later. Just turn 'round and start walkin'."

There wasn't nothing else to do in the face of a load of buckshot and six fellas all packing iron. We started walking back to our camp.

"How'd it happen?" I asked Sam.

"I don't know," he said. His voice was shaky, but whether with fear, anger, regret, or all three, I couldn't tell. "I just leaned back against the rock there and laid the shotgun right beside me. The next thing I knew, one of Mayfield's buddies grabbed my arms and Mayfield took the double-barrel. He fired a shot to get you to come out, and . . ."

"Those stinking robbers!" I said. "They did this to the Wild West, but they ain't gonna take the Monarch. We'll get guns and fight back!" I was hot; boiling mad. It wasn't just that they were stealing silver from me; they was stealing my Lark! If I'd had a gun right then, I would have gone back to do murder without another thought.

Dad Billou cleared his throat and waited for me to cool

down enough for him to speak. "Them fellas? Shoot you just for looking at 'em. Mayfield killed a sheriff. Ain't caught and hanged yet. Gonna face that?"

"But we can't just let them take it! Can't give up without a fight!"

Dad coughed again and said, "Live dog better than dead lion, reckon. More silver out there. Just go find another."

"Dad's right," Sam said. "If we went back they'd kill us. Then we still wouldn't have a mine and we'd be dead. Some day this territory will have law enough to take care of Mayfield and his kind, but not now."

I give it up then. My partners weren't going to back my play, and the truth was, I knowed they was right. I was no good to Lark dead. I reminded myself that I was precious little good to her living neither. I felt lower than low.

Dad said he was leaving that very day to go to prospecting again. Sam and me could have gone with him, but we didn't have the heart. Dad packed up his few things, wished us both luck, and took off down the trail toward the town of Bodie.

Sam and I sat and stared at the dirt or the sky; anywhere but at each other. Finally I could not stand it any more. "I gots to know," I said. "Was you asleep when they snuck up on you?"

"No," Sam said. "I was writing another letter to the newspaper." After a time of misery he asked, "So what do we do now, pard?"

I did not know if Sam was asking what we should do to make another fortune or if he meant that we should go set a spell and have a cup of coffee over the matter. The two of us did not have more than five dollars between us and just enough grub to whomp up something akin to Uncle Dimmy's Last Supper.

"Now that we are no longer rich men, I could use something to eat," I said to him.

"That is a start."

So I fixed our next to last pot of beans and throwed in our last bacon for flavor. We ate our supper without saying another word to one another for we was both feeling pretty low, what with Dad gone and the Monarch up the flume. Worse yet, my misery was on account of letting Lark down. I recollected what she said to me that day about how having hope, if it were false hope, would break her heart. All these months and I was no nearer to redeeming her. I was a failure in the one and only thing that mattered to me. I was like a cloud passing over a dry and thirsty land without yielding even one drop of rain.

Sam's misery was on account of the real probability that he might have to get hisself a job of some sort to stay alive. He lay beside the fire and smoked his last pipeful of tobacco.

"It's all finished for me now. I do not intend to go back home to Missouri to be pitied and mocked behind my back."

"No need. You can stay here and get the same treatment."

Another half hour passed before he spoke again. "I could clerk. That's it. I was a grocery clerk for a day back home. I could . . ."

"One day?" That seemed to be as long as Sam kept interest in anything.

"I ate up the proprietor's supply of stick candy, so I got the boot. I considered taking up the law profession, but that was wearisome. Once I was employed in a bookshop, but the customers continually interrupted my reading, so I left that position." He shook his head and tugged his beard, which was growed most down to the top button of his shirt. "I got two hundred and fifty dollars a month on the river, but nothing called a river around here runs a stream of water bigger than a pump spout." He sighed. "What are we to do, Jim? It's hard to think of working after being so wealthy. I am as worthless as some of those giant gopher holes the boys call mines out there."

He was pretty worthless alright. I had never seen a man who worked so hard at not working. But as he felt so bad already, I did not want to heap my scorn on his torment. Besides, I had my own list of failures to consider.

"We'll sleep on it," I said to Sam, and then I turned my back to him and the fire and hoped he would shut up. I laid awake and considered everything that had happened. It crossed my mind to try and get our claim back. Or suppose I broke my promise to Lark and come to steal her away?

But Lark was right about all that. I knowed the truth. Being a black man, I'd have been strung up from the nearest tree and left for the buzzards.

So I just passed that long night in grief and pining for my gal. As long as Lark was still in debt, then I was not a freeman neither. Thinking on these things was more work than working ever could be.

My soul grew weary with it. By and by I fell asleep and dreamed of silver strikes and marching up to pay off Lark's debt. Them was good dreams to see me through such a black night. When I come to, the sun was not up yet, but I could see a faint purple glow seeping through the clouds above the mountain. I thought that the pretty light was some sign of hope. It commenced to raining, but I was not put off.

It come to me that if me and Sam could strike it rich once, why not do it again?

"Sam!" I shook him awake.

"Leave me in peace," he moaned.

"Get up! There's plenty of silver to be had and gold too, if we'll just go dig for it!"

"What're you saying?" He pushed me back.

"If'n we found it once, why not again? Dad says he can do it. Ain't we as good as him? There's two of us and we is younger."

He was not altogether convinced. He pointed up at the sky and told me that winter was coming and that we would not have time to dig our own graves before the snows would come. All the same, I was sure of it. Sam was going to be a wealthy man and I would have my Lark! All we had to do was dig.

At last, hunger roused my partner out of his wallow, and we ate our cold beans and commenced to climbing far up that mountainside where I had seen the light breaking through the clouds. I took what I remembered from Dad Billou's lessons, found a likely spot, and we set to digging. Truth to tell, I went at it with a pick until a lot of dirt and rock was loosened up and there were a hole about eight feet deep.

"Big enough to bury us both," Sam said.

Then he climbed down in that hole with his long handle shovel to throw out the dirt. He hated the long handle shovel, Sam did. He still had not got the hang of it.

"Brace it forward and shove with the side of your knee 'til it is full, then throw it backwards over your shoulder . . ." I had showed him how a thousand times, but it didn't do no good.

He worked at it for awhile, tossed the gravel just on the edge of the hole and back it all come on his head and down his neck.

Sam did not say one word. He just clumb out of that shaft and marched on back down to the shanty where he give up all hope of living. I pitied him a mite. He was a sorry piece of humanity: could not hold a job, could not study the law, could not throw a shovelful of dirt out of a mine shaft without hitting himself in the head.

"I am useless," he moaned at last. "In all the world there is no more worthless man than myself. What am I fit for, Jim? What sort of an occupation can such an inept bag of wind as myself ever hope to hold?"

It was a tough problem, alright.

The answer to that very question, however, come the next morning in a letter from Virginia City. Sam opened it up and hollered, "Eureka!" which was what some folks said when they stuck their pick into the mother lode and drew out a big nugget. "This is a letter from Joe Goodman, editor of the *Territorial Enterprise*!" Sam flapped the sheet of paper beneath my nose and gave a whoop that made most of Aurora reach for their side arms. "My calling has called me at last! Mister Goodman likes my letters! He asks me to come to Virginia City and join the staff of his newspaper!"

To my thinking, this was the last hope of a desperate and hungry man. Sam had been offered twenty-five dollars a week with the *Territorial Enterprise* to work as a reporter in Virginia City.

"I'll never have to work again, Jim!" he cried joyfully. "I shall be a journalist!"

Chapter 10

Through timber claims and mine claims and odd jobs; through true hopes and false ones and expectations lifted and dashed, I had kept my word to Lark and had not ventured to Virginia City. But after Aurora fizzled I had to ask myself the question: What was I to do?

Dad Billou had up and deserted us. Now Sam headed northeast across the dusty valley toward Mount Davidson where the shanties, saloons, and hurdy-gurdy houses of "Virginny" perched on trembling ground above the warren of mine shafts. It seemed to me that I didn't have no choice in the matter, so I went along with him.

The clouds cleared off long about evening. Still a full fifty miles from our destination I looked up at the outline of that steep, treeless mountain rising seven thousand feet up, and I seen the glimmer of Virginia City's lights. It was altogether beautiful at such a distance.

The next day it was something else when we climbed the road. We passed through the rock pinnacles known as Devil's Gate and the dusty lawlessness of Gold Hill to come to the truth of the place: Mount Davidson was as steep as the tin roof on a Chinaman's wash house. The town roosted on that slope about halfways up the mountain between heaven and sulfurous perdition. The only thing that kept Virginia City from sliding on down to hell was the fact that the roads was terraced and braced. A man could walk into the front door of a west-facing building at street level, but by the time he reached the back side of the structure, the floor was supported by tall stilts. Out the back windows were a view of the rooftops and chimneys of his backdoor neighbor. Further than that were the mines and milling operations—smokestacks and tin buildings and hoisting works. Heaps of pulverized rocks from the diggings trailed away like the gravel of giant anthills. Beyond that, down Six Mile Canyon, a range of desolate mountains fell away into the same desert that me and Sam had crossed. It didn't look quite real from such a height. Beautiful it were, like glimpsing the Promised Land. I purely admired that view the first time I ever seen it and ever after.

There was a population of about eighteen thousand souls who lived there, most men. Twenty-four hours of the day at least one-third of them was underground working a shift in a mine. Wages for miners was world renowned. Men who never had two dollars to rub together was making the unheard-of sum of four dollars per day.

Nobody was a native of Nevada unless it was maybe a Paiute Indian or tiny babe what had the fortune to be born there. Every citizen of Virginia City had heard about the miracle of the Comstock and had come from distant lands to partake of that miracle. Every state and nation were represented: Chinese, Russians, Englishmen, Cornishmen, Irishmen, Frenchmen, Hungarian Jews, and Germans. In their homelands they most likely hated one another and their daddies had marched off to kill each other on a right regular schedule. On the boardwalks, the babble of blasphemy was in so many different languages and accents that it was positively biblical. They had all come on a pilgrimage to worship the silver god of the Comstock in their own language.

I reckon no place on earth had ever rose up out of the ground full-growed like that place. When I first laid my eyes upon it, Virginia City were a new town of fine brick buildings. There was a fire brigade, fire chief, mayor, aldermen, a sheriff, and a tribe of deputies. To accommodate all this grandness was a Masonic Lodge, Oddfellows Hall, hotels, banks, a half-dozen jails, whiskey mills every few paces, saloons, gambling palaces, hurdy-gurdy houses, a street full of Chinese, a few Paiute campodie huts on the fringe, and even a church or two in the midst.

The only instrument keeping track of all this confusion was the newspapers. The papers, which meant Sam, reported on the doings of all these establishments and all momentous events . . . parades, politics, processions, occasional visits by acting troupes and singers, brawls, murders, uprisings, riots, hangings, funerals, births, deaths, and of course the news of what was doing in the mines. Compared to all of this, the War between the States seemed almost of no account.

That may have been what some foreign folks thought about that far distant battle between North and South. The truth was that the Civil War was being fought hard right there in that town. And that great and terrible war would be won or lost according to what transpired right there in the Comstock. . . .

All of this bustle was already in full swing by the time me and Sam entered Virginia City that first morning. It were like a carnival. The boardwalks was so tight packed with people that it was hard for us to trudge against the tide. The dirt streets was just as busy. Teams of mules pulled ore wagons. Buckboards and buggies rattled up and down C Street. Crossing on foot was a positive peril.

I glanced down the slope that led to D Street where the soiled doves of Virginia City lived in small cabins. It was plain to see that men on their way back from the mines was enticed to stop awhile. The sight of miners peeling off to find their way down D Street made me feel a mite uneasy. Many of them women had begun their fall as hurdy-gurdy gals and had ended up living in a place like that.

I tried not to think on it no more when I spotted the sign of the Virginia Hotel. I hoped Lark was still there, yet I dreaded the fact that she might be still there.

Sam's mind was fixed on fighting through the crowds to get on down to the office of the *Territorial Enterprise*. Then, of a sudden, Sam stopped cold and nudged me hard.

"Look there!" He pointed back down the slope toward the D Street cribs, and I was afraid he had spotted Lark. Although I had not told Sam how I loved her, I was sure that he would remember her from the day she blowed into Carson.

But it weren't Lark or the ladies he was gawking at. There, tied up to a rail just where Chinatown started, was a whole string of twenty or so camels. Some of them was kneeling down and resting, chewing their cud just as peaceful as any milk cow. I had never seen such critters before except as pictures in the Good Book, so this was a fearful curious sight. Me and Sam was thunderstruck by the vision. Sam had heard in a letter from Orion that camels was being used to haul salt across the flats from the desert. When Sam had read the letter out loud, me and Dad Billou had laughed and thought that Orion had gone crazy or that he meant this as a joke. But Orion recounted the details about how the U.S. Army had bought them for thirty thousand dollars and brought them there to patrol the western vastness. They was not much use to the Union troops, so now they just trudged back and forth across the desert carrying their burdens. They scared horses and mules to death and was not well liked by the citizens of Storey County. They might not have been anything more than furry freight wagons, but they was miraculous to me and it took some time before I was willing to follow after Sam.

We come to the door of the *Territorial Enterprise*. He shook my hand and asked me what I intended to do. Without thinking, I blurted, "I'm going to visit down to the Virginia House Hotel."

His eyes got narrow and he give me a grin, which was his way of saying that he knowed what I was up to. "You gonna get drunk and have a dance with that little hurdy-gurdy gal?"

Now Sam knowed I did not drink tangleleg. Never a drop touched my lips since I was a child and lived with Uncle Dimmy. Nor did I hold with dancing, except the kind Uncle Dimmy had done in church when the Holy Ghost fell upon him.

"I just want to go see the place."

He give a laugh. "Well I do believe you're blushin', Jim Canfield."

"Ain't possible."

"That may be . . ." He smoothed his moustache. "I hear tell there is a beautiful black bird over there who sings like a lark . . . You talk in your sleep, you know."

I give a shrug like it didn't matter and told him to mind his own business. After this he said to me that I ought to mind mine as well because everyone in Nevada knew the sort of men who hung around Virginia Hotel. By this he meant the rebel sympathizers who had pledged their oath to the Confederacy. He also told me not to look any man of them in the eyes lest I get myself shot and lynched and afterwards killed. Those types did not cotton to free blacks, not even in the West.

I thanked him for his care, then he went on into the newspaper office. I felt mighty alone. He was the most lazy and shiftless man I had ever knowed, but he was likable and I had grown accustomed to seeing after him.

So there I stood on the edge of that muddy boardwalk. I stared at the outside of the Virginia Hotel hoping to see some glimpse of Lark through a window. But I did not see her even at a distance. It were quite awhile before I crossed the street and walked back the other direction. I considered that just being there was breaking a promise to her. Maybe there was some way to see her where she would not see me. Then I put my hand up to my face. I had a full beard and my clothes was the rough, blousy red shirt of a miner. My pants was tucked into muddy boots, and I was all over in need of a good bath, brush, and curry.

"Even if Lark sees you, she ain't gonna know you," I said to myself. I felt in disguise and was glad of the mud.

As I walked on, piany music tumbled out the doors of

every saloon. Though it were not yet noon, men bellied up to the bars and gathered round the faro tables to buck the tiger and lose their hard-earned pay. Businesses was open round the clock to accommodate the three shifts in the mines. A man could get off work at six in the morning, drink a bottle of tarantula juice before seven, dance with a girl at seven-thirty, lose what was left of his wages by eight, and still get plenty of sleep before he had to go back to work that night.

I walked past all that. A white man grabbed up a China-man by his pigtail and flung him off the boardwalk. Nobody paid no mind but me. Just ahead a drunk got throwed out of a saloon. He laid there on the planks and three men stepped over him. I stopped just long enough to drag him off and prop him against the wall.

A man in a checkered coat and trousers laughed at me and said, "New around here, ain't you? You'll never get anywhere if you stop and pick up every drunk. Care to play a little five-card draw?"

I thanked him kindly and pressed on.

As the piany music played, it was accompanied by a deep bass booming in the bowels of the mountain as miners blasted away in the shafts. The earth trembled beneath my feet, and I half expected the ground to open and swallow up the whole of Virginia City in one eruption of fire and brimstone. Along with all this business was a roar from the mills and mines that sounded like thunder and cannons all in one.

Then in the rabble and the crush and the noise I spotted Lark a half block up the way. Her high-collared dress was the color of wine. She had a cape around her shoulders and a black felt bonnet on her head. I could make out her profile: long lashes, high cheek bones, full mouth. If anything, she was more beautiful than I ever thought a woman could be. She was standing just outside the window of the Kroeger's Drygoods store and looking through the glass at what was on display.

I stopped dead in my tracks and pulled my slouch hat down lower over my brow. Someone bumped into me, then another, but I did not budge 'til she went into that building.

Sneaking up on the place easylike, I peeked through the window to see what she was looking at: a pale blue satin bonnet with flowers on it—daisies. It were the kind of thing a lady would wear out on a drive in a buggy with her favorite beau. I thought to myself, "Now this is what Lark was gazing at. She'd like to have that bonnet." I wondered if she come to this store often and how long she had been wanting that bonnet.

My whole heart begun to ache, and I wanted to rush on in there and take her in my arms and hold her against me like I had been thinking about for months. But I did not do that. Dumb and dirty, I stood there outside that glass and looked in at her the way she had looked at that bonnet. And there was some pleasure in the looking and the wanting. There was some filling of the empty place in my soul where only she could fit.

She bought some fabric, red-and-black-checked, and some thread and needles. The clerk, a mousy little man, did not smile back at her when she said some friendly word to him. I saw her smile fade away. She looked out the window, right at me. Away she turned, then quick back again.

She studied on me for a heartbeat, and then her face filled with amazement. She recognized me under the mud!

I started to run, but she was out the door and hollering my name. "Jim! . . . Jim!"

I took a few more steps and ducked round the corner of the building. She followed. Next thing I knowed she were glaring at me.

"Howdy, Lark." I took off my hat.

"What you doin' here?" She was riled.

"Claim got jumped . . . gotta get work . . ."

I begun to babble on about Sam and Dad Billou and how we almost had it!

There was no hope for her redemption in them words. I was just as bust as any poor miner on the Comstock. I would have to go down in the shafts if I could even get hired. Four dollars a day. Six if I got lucky. Where was hope for her redemption in that?

I seen the light drain out of her eyes. I knowed she had been dreaming of me as much as I had been of her. But dreams were not going to buy her freedom.

"I come to get you," I blurted.

She put her fingers on my mouth. "Hush now. Not another word like that. They'll kill you and make no mistake! Get out of Virginny."

"Not without you." I started toward her.

She pushed me away as some dude walked by without hardly noticing us. Then the fellow turned around to look back.

Lark said in a loud, brassy tone. "You want to spend time with me it'll cost you plenty, honey!" Then she whispered in a voice so full of pain I thought she would break and me too. "Don't try to see me. Please, Jim! I loves you and they'll kill you if they know it! Don't . . . don't, Jim! You don't know how it really is!" One warm touch on my brow. At that she turned and fled back to the Virginia Hotel.

I was feeling as low as I ever had, watching her go. After that I stood beside the window of the drygoods store and gazed down at the satin bonnet and thought of her in it and me sitting beside her in the best buggy at Green Freight and Livery.

Dreams . . . vapor . . . nothing at all.

I left to find me some place to sleep out of the cold.

———•••———

"Can't use you," the mine superintendent said, turning his back on me and walking away for the third day in a row. It had nothing to do with a lack of work; only because I was black. That was enough to get me sent to the back of the line of men waiting for employment at the Mexican Mine. It didn't matter if I stayed there all night and was the first one at the foreman's office window the next morning. As long as there was one white man looking for work, I got set back behind him and behind the next that come, and so forth, till another day had passed.

What with winter coming on, Virginia City's mines had plenty of workers to choose from. When the weather turned cold, lots of fellas who thought they was prospectors just naturally headed toward finding work that will keep them warm and fed. Four dollars a day was what the mines was paying, but not to me. It wasn't just the Mexican, neither. The story was the same at the Ophir, the Gould and Curry, and all the rest.

Sam saw to it that I got shelter and grub, but that couldn't keep on forever. He was just getting started as a reporter and his twenty-five dollars didn't stretch awful far. Even he was sharing cramped quarters with Dan DeQuille and other newspapermen.

I was living way below D Street, down in Chinatown. Had a pallet on the floor in the back room of Sing Woo's laundry. Sam talked his boss, Joe Goodman, into giving the laundry free advertising in the paper, in exchange for the tin roof over my head and three bowls of rice a day. Goodman was a staunch Union man, and Sam explained how we had lost our claim in the Monarch to some rebels.

Goodman also had the newspaper's Chinese cook feed me some. If not for that and Sam buying me meals besides, I would have plumb starved to death. But it could not keep on that way. I had to get work. I was not able to even help myself, let alone help Lark.

Joining the day shift from the mine that just got off work, I trudged along C Street toward the brick building that was the newspaper office. Noyes, the printer's devil, give me a big hello, and shouted over the noise of the press that Sam was in his office.

He meant that Sam was across the street in the Delta Saloon, but I met him out in the street. He could tell from my face that I had still had no luck finding work. "Jim," he said to me, "I've been giving your situation some thought, and I think I know the answer."

I looked off toward the flag fluttering over the top of Mount Davidson and thought how if this was a joke, I'd strangle him. "Tell me," I said.

"Tomorrow morning, you go up to the superintendent

and tell him you'll work for nothing." He stood there grinning with his eyes and moustache the way he always did, like he'd said something really clever.

"Sam, I ain't in the mood for none of your . . ."

"I'm not joking," he said. "You tell Superintendent Duncan, or whoever, that you love to work; can't live without it, and that you'll work for free, for the pure enjoyment of it. He'll hire you on the spot just to see if you're serious."

"How do that help me? I still don't gets no pay that way."

"That's not the end of the scheme. Listen: You not only work for nothing, you work harder than anybody, the way I saw you swing the pick down in Aurora. Word will get around, and people will start pointing you out and asking the foreman about you. By the end of the week, two at the outside, the foreman and the superintendent will be so embarrassed that they'll offer to pay you. But don't you take it."

"No?"

"No! Because by then you'll be famous. Other mine superintendents will be bidding for your services. They'll all want to have the famous Jim Canfield working for them."

"How am I gonna get famous so fast?"

"Because I'm going to write a story about you for the paper that will make you sound like Hercules and Atlas and Samson all rolled up together!"

And that is exactly what happened.

Chapter 11

I was down at the six-hundred-foot level of the Mexican Mine. We was opening a new chamber, working along a drift, and once again I was half of a double-jack team. It might seem that swinging a ten-pound sledge for eight hours straight was no cause for rejoicing, but I was right proud of myself. When I was working for nothing, like Sam had suggested, miners stopped to watch. Pretty soon they was bringing their friends by to look, even men off-shift from other mines coming down to see if it was true.

There was some grousing at first amongst the diggers what had rebel sentiments, about me being black, but even that stopped when they seen how hard I was working for nothing. The crew boss, Irish fella name of Mackay, took special pride in me on account of how when I joined his level it started moving more rock than any two other teams. He took it on hisself to talk to Superintendent Duncan personal about getting me some pay.

It took ten days, but Duncan had finally give in and offered to pay me. Seeing how the *Enterprise* was making special mention of the Mexican Mine and him in particular as being the proprietor of such a curiosity as me, what else could he do? What clinched it was when the superintendent of the Chollar Mine offered me six dollars a day to go to work for him, for the bragging rights I guess. I was relieved when Duncan said he'd beat that offer by fifty cents a day, in order to keep me. Besides, Boss Ward was still over at the Chollar, and the last thing I wanted was to work anywheres near him.

There was a Cousin Jack, which is what Cornishmen was called, working on the same level with me. Him and me partnered up to work the double jack. Truro was a square-built man and tough. His arms was most big around as other men's legs. His given name was Bodmin, which around Virginny was soon corrupted to "Bad Man," so Bad Man Truro was how the Comstock knew him. Such a nickname often got him into fights with those who wanted to try on the man behind the name, which was odd for two reasons. First off, he was as mild a man as could be and would never have picked a fight with no one. And second, he always won. He'd stand his ground whilst the challenger got in a couple licks that he felt no more than if hit with a feather. Then Truro would wrap the fella up in a bear hug and squeeze until the other party either give up or passed out.

We was sitting a hundred feet inside the drift, just at the bottom of a winze, a slope leading upwards to the level above. It was a spot with a nice breeze blowing through for us to stop and have our midshift meal. Truro wiped the dust off his face with a neckerchief. I stuck my candlestick into the square-set timber overhead and we both opened our pails.

"And what have you got today?" Truro asked me.

Now this was a good question, since I was still picking up meals from the newspaper's Chinese cook. He always fixed American vittles, but he sometimes slipped in a Chinese treat as well. On this occasion, it was dried shrimp.

"What unholy thing is that?" Truro scowled in disgust. "You've taken to heathen ways for certain if you'll eat the husks of bugs!"

"He give me these before," I said, popping a shrimp in my mouth. "Try one?"

"Not me; never," he vowed. "Only good Christian food for me!" Here he took out a block of yellow cheese, a handful of crackers and a jug of black tea. Before he carved himself a hunk of cheese, he crumbled a cracker into a chipped saucer and poured a little tea over it, then he set it on a small ledge in front of a clay doll.

"Tell me again what you call that thing."

"It's a tommyknocker," he replied, "or the form of one."

The six-inch-tall seated figure wore a peaked cap, had busted-off match heads in its face for eyes and the stump of a real clay pipe clenched in its grinning mouth. It looked odd, sitting there on the rock face in the flickering candlelight; not evil, but mischievous. "You ain't worshipping no idol?" I teased.

"Not a bit of it," Truro said. "I learned of them from my own father, who worked the tin mines in the old country. Tommyknockers are only wee spirits that play games with miners like hiding tools and blowing out candles. But it is wise to be kind to them, since they rap on the walls to warn of cave-ins."

"Truro," I said, "do you really think some fairy will come out here and eat them crackers?"

"No," he agreed. "It is probably just the rats growing fat on easy pickings. But you never know. Down here in the belly of the earth, we need all the good luck we can muster."

I agreed with that. It didn't pay to think too hard on having wooden timbers holding up six hundred feet of rock over your head. Or how pitch-dark it was when the candles did blow out.

"Did you hear we'll be getting a new shift boss? Meanest man on the Comstock, or so they say," Truro remarked around a mouthful of crackers.

"How so?"

"Makes the men work in air so hot and foul that they pass out. Says if they can stand up, they can keep working. Hard driver, he is, and will give a man notice for going to the water barrel without permission. Killed a man too."

"A miner?"

Truro nodded, remembering the story. "Welshman, it was. Seems the boss ordered him to go into a drift full of steam and the miner refused. The shift boss cursed him and give the man a shove, then the Welshman took a swing. The foreman was ready for him though, because he always carries a sawed-off drill about two feet long. Cracked the Welshman's head like an egg."

"And this shift boss walked away clean?"

"Coroner said it was self-defense."

"And he's coming to work here? What's his name?"

Truro tied the bandana back around his forehead to keep the sweat from running into his eyes as we got set to go back to work. "I heard his name from a cousin of mine who works at the Chollar. My cousin said we were welcome to him too. Now if I could just recall . . ."

"From the Chollar," I repeated, feeling a sudden dread. "Is his name Ward?"

"That's it exactly," Truro agreed.

———•·•·•———

Even though I was finally making good, steady wages, I kept my little room back of Sing Woo's laundry so as to save every cent for Lark.

Six days a week I labored. On the seventh day I counted up my savings, which come to thirty-six dollars each week after I took out three dollars a week for expenses like eating, which cost me fifty cents a day for six days. I skipped grub altogether on Sundays and set my mind on things above while I put aside an additional four bits a week.

By the end of four months I had over six hundred dollars in the bank. This didn't sound like much until I figured that in three years I would have the sum I needed to get my gal free. I dreamed only of that.

Then, one afternoon on the coldest day of winter, something happened that changed my life forevermore. I suppose it would not be too strong to say that on down the line that small event might have even changed the course of something as important as the war between the North and South.

I was coming back to Sing Woo's when I spied a bright silver dollar laying half stuck between two planks on the boardwalk. I stopped for a minute and looked around to see who might own it, but I didn't see nobody else so I grabbed it up with rejoicing.

From just round the corner of the alley I heard Truro holler, "Jim, so you've had a bit of luck. Come on up with me and the lads and give the roulette wheel a spin on that lucky dollar you've just found."

For a minute I considered it, although I did not hold with gambling. Temptation reared up mighty powerful in me. But I did not yield to it.

"No, thank-you kindly," I said.

"Then come have a drink with me. Just to be sociable."

"No, thank-you kindly, Truro."

"At least come pay your dollar and listen to that little Lark gal sing for awhile."

Now this stopped me in my tracks. I looked at that shiny new coin and wondered if it had not fell from heaven just so I could sit a spell in the dance hall of the Virginia Hotel and rest my eyes on Lark and hear her sing. But then I thought about what would happen if I was to find one stray silver dollar every week. Why that would mean fifty-two a year! A tidy sum.

"No, thank-you kindly, Truro," I said.

Somebody else behind of me hollered, "What'cha gonna do with that, Jim?"

"Put it in the bank," I told him.

It was this kind of thing that had give me the reputation of a miser. Folks talked all around about how I hoarded my cash up in the Bank of California. They talked about how I was the man who worked for no pay at all, and now that I had wages, I never spent so much as a dime on the good life. Money meant nothing to me, they said. They figured I didn't care about a thing at all in life except working.

Well, they was wrong. I did not tell them that I cared for someone more dearly than my own life. They talked about the hurdy-gurdy gals down at the Virginia Hotel.

Every Saturday night Truro asked why I did not go on up there and listen to that little songbird, since we was of the same kind? I just pretended like it did not interest me. Truth was, I often debated something terrible inside myself whether I ought to squander one dollar just to be near her for an hour, or save that dollar to buy her contract.

While the other men rushed to lose their cash in the cribs of D Street or the saloons and gambling palaces of C Street, I put that dollar I found in my pocket with every intention of having supper, washing up, then going up to deposit it.

I prayed that I would see her when I was out and about Virginia City. Sometimes I walked past the Virginia Hotel at the time I knowed she would be singing and I slowed way down and fussed with getting gravel out of my boots so I could hear her without getting into a brawl with the bouncer for loitering.

On the times when Lark and me did meet by accident, she was cool to me and I was tongue-tied. I figured she had stopped loving me the way a wildcat miner stops loving a false vein of silver when it plays out after a few feet.

I did not blame her, but I knowed she would feel different once I let my true purpose be known.

So, let folks call me miser. I didn't care a pin for it. All I cared for was putting that silver dollar into my pocket and then in the bank with the rest of my dollars so they might be fruitful and multiply.

On that cold day, there was snow on the mountains and a frigid wind begun to wail down from the top of Mount Davidson. I lowered my head against the cold and paid no mind to my companions as they trekked on toward the C Street saloons to warm themselves.

Passing the fallow garden patch of Sing Woo, I noticed someone hunkered down and diggin' in that near frozen field. His back was to me. I could see he was a big man and it was plain that he was hungry. He give a happy little whoop and held up a scrawny turnip like he had found a sack of gold. Curious, I walked toward him and hollered so as he would not think I had come to rob him of his turnip.

"Howdy," I said in a friendly tone. "I didn't know there was any turnips left in Sing Woo's patch."

He quick stuck the pitiful vegetable into his pocket and jumped to his feet. Facing me, he looked like a grizzly bear: big, hairy, mean-eyed, ready to pounce. His clothes was dirty, but not ragged. His cheek was swollen and blue under his right eye. He looked to be in his early thirties.

He growled at me, "This here is my turnip. Don't matter who owns this plot! It would have just gone to seed if'n I hain't found it."

I smiled. "Sing Woo don't mind. Keep it. Just that I ain't seen you round these parts, that's all. Seems a man's gotta be mighty hungry to go scrounging round in a turnip patch for his supper."

"I ain't et in four days." He relaxed some. "Got jumped and robbed just this side of Six Mile Canyon. It were dark as pitch. I made my camp. They pistol-whipped me, took my money, stole my horse, kicked me forty feet down an abandoned mine shaft and left me to starve. I got out though, and after I eat this turnip I'm goin' after the bunch what done it."

"You know who done it?"

He begun to walk back with me toward Sing Woo's place. "Not zactly. Their faces was covered, but I'll find them when I find my horse."

I told him my name and shook his hand.

"They call me Kettle Belly Brown," he said, rubbing his hand on a belly that were indeed big like a kettle. "I come from Missouri." He looked me over real good. "I don't reckon you're a secesh?"

I laughed. "Not last time I checked. But the woods are full of 'em hereabouts. A man can't hardly walk without steppin' on a Copperhead here in Virginny."

He brushed off the turnip and put the whole thing in his mouth in one bite. He kept talking while he chewed. "That's what I heard . . . secesh . . . Copperheads . . . all over the Comstock. Most as many as any place except them that rides with Jeb Stuart, I hear."

"They don't cause no trouble out here."

At that he nearly choked on his turnip. "Well, I aim to catch me a certain reb."

I asked him to come in for a real meal—One of Sing Woo's Chinese dinners. Sing Woo did not like Kettle Belly from first look, however. He said right out in plain pidgin, "Stink! Stink like pig. You don' eat 'less you go wash. You don' eat 'less you pay now!"

"I reckon I'll have wind soup and snowflake stew for supper then," Kettle Belly turned his pockets out to show they was empty.

"One charity case enough!" Little Sing Woo, who weren't but half the size of Kettle Belly, gave the big man a shove. Sing Woo shook his finger at me. "You bad enough! Cheap! Miser! All the time pay me nothing! Why now you bring hungry tiger for Sing Woo feed! Pay my one dollah or you don' eat!"

I put my hands in my pockets and backed off from Sing Woo. He had hit me with a washboard once before because I did not roll up my pallet in the morning. He was small but tough as a banty rooster.

I felt the dollar in my pocket. I don't know what come over me, but I pulled out that dollar and held it up for Sing Woo to see. "There's your dollar, you little Chinese pirate! Now shut your trap and go fix us something to eat. This man is been robbed and pillaged enough. He is near to dying with hunger! So git!"

Sing Woo's eyes widened. "You! Where you get that? Cheap! How come you never pay Sing Woo dollah for meal before?" Snatching the coin from my hand, he went back in the laundry and hollered out, "Pig! Pig! Go wash or no eat!"

So we washed up while he cooked up the biggest platter of Chinese grub I had ever seen. Kettle Belly was so hungry that he just ate the whole heap without commenting on the way it looked. While he wolfed down his food, he told me the story of how he had come to leave Missouri and go west.

On his mother's side, Kettle Belly was kin to old John Brown, who had tried to free the slaves and got himself hanged and nearly started the war single-handed.

I thought to myself that if old John Brown were anything at all like Kettle Belly Brown, then the old man must have swung his sword of retribution with a mighty rage against the slavers.

Seems that in all the battling back and forth in them

days of the massacres at the Kansas border, the wife and sister of Kettle Belly got in the way of reb bullets and was killed. He knowed the voice of the man who done it during a midnight raid, but not the face. Since the fateful day of the killing, he had set out on a trail of revenge against the murderer and the trail had led him west to Virginia City.

"He's finished when I lay my hands on him." He bit through the bone of a pork rib. "He thinks he's gonna get shed of me by hiding out in these mines, but he's done for. By the time I get through with him he'll beg for mercy and that's a fact. Not only has he murdered my loved ones . . ." His words trailed off like he had thought of something and almost said it when he was not supposed to.

It were a sad story and I pitied him, but I didn't ask him no more about it. It were plain that he was nearly eat up inside with hating this faceless reb and wanting revenge on his life.

I had seen such things before. Sometimes hate kept a man alive, but eat him up inside at the same time. Most likely it were hate that helped Kettle Belly to climb out of that mine and then stagger up the mountain to where I found him, but to what end? It were better, I thought, not to talk about it no more for fear of it boiling over right then and there.

It was late afternoon when we finished eating. Whilst I went out to bring in an armload of wood for the stove, Kettle Belly took off his filthy clothes, wrapped himself in a blanket, laid down on my pallet, and fell fast asleep. Snored like a hog too.

Sing Woo heard the snorting and stormed into the back room. He shook his finger at Kettle Belly and tried to get another dollar out of me if the giant was going to room with me. I told him if he threw out a man who had just been robbed and beat up, then he had no kind of heart.

"That's right! Sing Woo got no kind heart! Sing Woo businessman! If big man stay, people think Sing Woo keep pigs in back room! They no bring laundry!"

He had a point, but I threatened him all the same. "I will speak to Sam about Sing Woo's cousin who is cook at the paper and I will get the cousin fired. Then Sing Woo will have to support him and there will be no profit in it!"

Sing Woo muttered Chinese curses at me, but he gathered up Kettle Belly's clothes to launder and left the poor man to sleep off his ordeal and the Chinese dinner.

———•◆•———

I ducked my head against the Washoe Zephyr that was blowing rain straight into my face. Even with my hat pulled low and tied in place with a bandana, the drops still smacked hard enough to sting.

Pulling up in the lee of the *Enterprise* office, I reckoned to stop in and visit Sam for a minute before chancing the waterfall that passed for the road down to Sing Woo's.

As fast as I could, I got inside and slammed the door shut again, but not before a whole chorus of yells erupted from the newspaper folk. "Close that! Hey, where'd page three blow off to? Keep that cussed thing shut! Bolt it!"

I stamped my boots to knock loose some of the mud before I tracked it all over the office, then untied the bandana and looked around. That room looked like a whole herd of crazy spiders had taken up residence. The roof leaked in more spots than the alphabet has letters. To keep the water from dripping on their precious compositions, the reporters had stuck tacks in next to each leak, then run strings down to tin cups, buckets, and pails. Just to go across the room without running foul of that web took a mess of navigation.

"Where's Sam?" I asked Dan.

"In the basement. He thinks it's drier down there. Course, he doesn't know how the flood waters are rising." This last comment was uttered in a voice loud enough to be heard below stairs, just so's Sam would hear.

"Whoever wants me, come on down." Sam's words floated up to me from below.

I found him bent over a desk with a pocketknife in his hand. He was slicing out columns from Eastern papers like the *New York Tribune* and the *Boston Globe*. "Jim!" he said. "Welcome. Come in and set. I'm almost through picking out the articles we'll reprint tomorrow."

He flung the remains of the *Tribune's* front page on to the floor and uncovered the desk blotter. It was a mass of scars, cuts, and slashes from the enthusiasm he brought to his work.

"Anything of note?" I asked.

"More of the same," he replied. "Lincoln's fired another general. He still can't locate anybody to stand up against Lee."

"Any of that war affect the Territory?"

He plumped down in a chair and frowned. "I've been giving that some thought. Foreign correspondents are full of how close Britain is to selling arms to the Confederacy. It seems that they are just waiting for two things."

"Which are?"

"Reports claim that Britain wants to see if the rebs can win a big victory on Northern soil . . . push the thing to a finish, you see."

"That surely could not have anything to do with us way out here."

"No, but the second condition does. England still wants proof that the South has money enough to come shopping at their store . . . real money, not paper . . . which means the Confederacy needs . . ."

"Virginia silver and California gold," I finished for him.

Sam nodded. "And not just picking off a stagecoach here and a single shipment there, but the whole output of the mines."

"Anybody back in the States figure this out yet?"

"Publisher Horace Greeley says Lee is planning a big campaign north to give the South its major victory. He also says that with so much attention focused on the threat from Lee, nobody will think about protecting us way out here. Maybe both things will happen at once."

"Has this Greeley convinced anybody yet?" I asked.

"Only one I know of," Sam said gloomily. "Me." He opened his poke of tobacco and thumbed a palmful into the bowl of his meerschaum. When he pulled a small pencil-sized object out of his waistcoat pocket and begun to tamp the load, I jumped over the desk and snatched it out of his hand.

"Don't you know what this is?" I asked with alarm.

"Found it on the street this morning," he said with shake of his head. "Why?"

"It's a blasting cap, you dunderhead. One good tamp

too many and you'll be counting your fingers by subtracting the ones in the next county!"

"Oh," he said. "In that case I won't use it as a pipe tool. I'll just keep it as a lucky piece."

I never did know if he was really that careless, or just playing the fool with me.

Chapter 12

The work in the mines went on, unrelieved by little in the way of entertainment. I still would not part with so much as a dollar that could be set aside toward Lark's redemption.

Amongst all the rest of the population of Virginia City, the favorite entertainment was gambling. The miners bet on most any kind of sporting proposition, so long as there would be one clear winner. They staged wrestling matches, fancy shooting exhibitions, and jumping contests between bullfrogs brought up from the river. There was competitions between teams of men drilling with double jacks and drinking marathons where the winner was the one still standing after guzzling bottles of Twenty Rod whiskey.

For a time the hands-down favorite was the dogfights. These was carried out in a big room downstairs below the Sazerac saloon. There was a circular pit, with wooden walls and floor, and space all around the outside for the spectators to stand. Men come from all over the territory with their snarling and vicious mutts, everyone eager to prove that his beast could take on all comers.

But after a space, even the excitement of that bloody

sport wore off. The simple, honest miners had been gulled into thinking that the contests were on the level, that the best dog won. Then one night one of the promoters was seen dousing the ruff of the favorite with something from a small blue bottle. He claimed it was liniment, but the suspicions of the boys was aroused.

They told the gambler they wanted to see him rub it on the challenger dog's coat too. When he refused, they give him the choice of either that or drinking it. Well, that busted up the contest. It seems that the professional handler had been dosing his dog's fur with strychnine, right where the opposing critter would take hold.

That promoter was give a brand-new suit of tar and feathers and rid out of town on a rail. He did not seem to appreciate the honor, though. Anyway, that experience soured the boys on dogfights and left them hankering for a new and novel way to lose their cash.

One night Truro come by where I was staying and wanted me to go with him to the Sazerac. He said there was an announcement being made there of a new entertainment. Right away, Kettle Belly said he'd like to go.

I didn't gamble, of course, being too tightfisted with my dollars to risk even one on the chance of winning more. But just then Sam stopped by. It seemed he had the same thing on his mind, and he was dressed to impress folks what were newly arrived in town. Ever since being made the editor in charge of local doings, or what they called "the local," Sam tried to look the part. That evening he wore a bright green necktie inside a gold-colored waistcoat, and his hair was slicked back with a pomatum that smelled of lilac water.

"Come along with us, Jim," he urged. "This new idea

is said to be a Goliath among sporting events—a real sock-dolager."

I could not see the harm in tagging along to hear what was being announced, so I agreed to accompany the other three to the Sazerac. At the time, it did not seem suspicious to me that every one of my friends showed up at once.

When we arrived at the saloon, the place was already packed out to the street. But Sam announced in a real loud voice, "Press! Make way for the *Enterprise,* boys. I've got to get the story straight for tomorrow's edition."

And the miners parted for him like the Red Sea done for Moses. Truro, Kettle Belly, and me swum along after, straight to the stage. Already up there was a fight promoter, a swell by the name of Hobie Piper, who liked to refer to hisself as an "impressario." Beside him was the little Arab fella who had accompanied the first shipment of camels to the U.S. back in the fifties and then stayed on. What his right name was, nobody could pronounce, so he went by the handle of Hi Jolly.

Piper motioned for quiet and when the buzz slacked off, begun his pitch. "My friends," he said, "The greatest kings the world has ever known were the fabulously wealthy sheiks and sultans of the mysterious deserts. Now those men, who could buy and sell the likes of Virginia City and command all the wealth of the Levant, had a favorite sport to which they were even more addicted than gold. Do you know what that was?"

"Harems?" Sam called out. Five minutes of laughter went on before the group settled down. Just when it would start to get calm, some latecomer would ask his neighbor what a harem was and the ruckus would start again.

"No, no!" Piper finally admonished the crowd into silence. "The most excellent of all pastimes, straight out of the marvels of the Arabian Nights, the sport for which sheiks would part with all the wealth of the Indies, was . . ." and he paused for the drama to build up, "camel racing!"

If the earlier joke had set the walls of the Sazerac to shaking, this declaration touched off a chorus that was like to raise the roof. "Them things?" was the shout. "Horses built by congressional committee! Spare parts left over from creation!"

Newfangled ideas always do take some time to get accepted. "Now here's the game," Piper continued, unfazed by the mocking. "I have hired the use of Hi Jolly's string, ten prime ships of the desert in top-notch racing form, to be used in a contest one week from Saturday. The prize will be one thousand dollars."

All of a sudden my head swum and the room seemed to spin. A thousand dollars? One-fifth of what I needed to redeem Lark, for winning one race? I begun to get excited, but my emotions plunged the next second.

"The entry fee will be one hundred fifty dollars per rider. I will naturally be giving odds and entertaining your bets as race time approaches." I half turned toward the door, not wanting to hear more. One hundred fifty dollars? It was crazy to even consider.

Sam caught me by the arm. "Is it true that the first rider to pay his fee gets first choice of the camels?" he yelled to Piper.

"Quite right," Piper agreed.

"Well then, here's your first entrant, Jim Canfield!"

"But, but . . ." I stammered.

"You are the best hand with a team I ever saw," Sam said. "There is no beast with four hooves that you can't master. Truro and Kettle Belly and I believe in you. We put up the money and you be the jockey. What do you say?"

What could I say? I shook hands with my friends, who had somehow nosed out the secret announcement beforehand and hoodwinked me into coming. The money was paid over and I stepped up on the stage.

———•◦•◦•———

What I had not known the night I was volunteered as a jockey in the first ever Virginia City camel race was that Sam had finagled his way to an inside track. Before even deciding to invest in me, Sam did a little snooping. From an hour's conversation with Hi Jolly, Sam discovered that one of the camels, Daisy by name, was by far the strongest and most likely runner. By being first up with the deposit, Sam had guaranteed our use of her for the race.

"Ain't that cheating?" I protested.

"Not at all," Sam responded, sounding shocked. "I just did a little journalistic research. Anyone else in the room could have stepped forward, same as us. That applies to the other . . . advantage . . . I have secured."

"What other advantage?" I asked drily.

"We have hired the services of Hi Jolly to be your exclusive trainer from now 'til race time. Every spare minute you have I expect you to be practicing."

So I come to learn the ways of riding camels from nearly the only fella in ten thousand miles who could teach it proper.

"Most riders will not know how to manage their beast

with only one rein," Hi told me. "They will try to hook up two, as with a horse, but this will only confuse the animal. And when a camel is confused he will not race."

"Sensible," I said. "Same thoughts as me. How do I steer with only one line?"

"Oh, you must carry a stick like so," he said, offering me a broom handle. "The rein offers only little control. The stick is used to give direction by tapping lightly on the side of the animal's face opposite the route desired and saying hut-hut-hut . . ."

"Uh-huh," I said. "Or uh-hut. And I'm going to learn this in one week?"

"No," Hi said. "Daisy already knows how to do all this. You are going to learn how to stay on."

At least he was being truthful.

I got my introduction to Daisy that same day. She was seven feet tall at the withers and weighed three-quarters of a ton. Covered with coarse brown fur on her hump, neck, and shoulders, she was lighter tan-colored on the rest of her. When I come into the paddock she swung her neck round to face me and chewed her cud thoughtfully.

"A very good sign," Hi said. "If she did not like you, she would have shown it."

"How's that?"

"She might have spit in your eye, or she might have chased you out of the pen while trying to bite you. She would not allow anyone she did not trust to be this near her baby."

That's when I first noticed the buckskin-colored small version of mama that snuggled up next to her on the far side. He peeked around behind her to look at me, then ducked his head back, shy.

"His name is Sultan. Daisy will run all the faster in the race to get back to him."

I coaxed Sultan to me with a handful of grain and soft words. He hung back at first, but soon enough I had him nibbling out of my palm. He let me scratch under his chin and made baby camel sounds of happiness, mostly bawling and grunting. Next thing I knowed, Daisy's big brown head was laid across my shoulder, and she batted her long eyelashes with maternal pride. I was accepted.

We spent the week practicing hut-hut-hut. Learning to ride that pack frame that passes for a saddle was tougher than I expected and I ate my share of red rock dust; but by the end of the seven days, I was ready.

The day of the race was a fine spring morning, with a cold breeze blowing off the Sierras and the Stars and Stripes snapping proudly in the wind on top of Mount Davidson. The contest was set to be run at noon and the start signal would be the midday blast of the Ophir Mine whistle whose works was closest to the course.

For want of an actual track, the camels was to race south down C Street to the firehouse at the far end of town, around it, and back to the starting point. The distance was about two miles.

I was already mounted up. Truro and Kettle Belly stood by Daisy's nose, keeping her calm. Sam, as befitted the promoter of our entry, was up in the stands, placing last-minute bets and acting the part of a nabob. I heard a rustle of silk and spotted Lark in the stands with some other ladies. I did not dare wave, but I do believe I seen her smile at me.

Truro joshed me some, when he seen where I was looking, but Kettle Belly's attention was elsewhere. Three entries further along was Ryeman, him who owned Lark's contract. I thought, not for the first time, how he reminded me of someone I had seen somewheres besides Virginia City, but there was no time to think on it then. The Virginia House and Ryeman also sponsored a rider, and it was no secret that the jockey was a secesh. The Copperheads was vocal about not letting a black man beat a true son of the South. Ryeman was giving his fella instructions in a loud and exasperated tone as their camel danced around in a circle.

"Hold him still, blast you!" I heard Ryeman yell. All at once, Kettle Belly disappeared.

"Hey!" I hollered, but right then the steam whistle shrilled and we was off!

Daisy jumped into the lead right away. We was followed by the entry of the Excelsior Volunteer Fire Company, the Knights of Columbus critter, and then the Virginia Hotel beast.

We made the first turn onto C Street proper, flying past the hoisting words of the Ophir and the Howling Wilderness saloon. Throwing a quick look after my competition, I seen the Knights of Columbus animal refuse the turn altogether and carry his hapless jockey up the slope toward the tailings dump of the Andes mine.

Past the International Hotel and the Bucket of Blood and on by the Delta saloon, the race still belonged to Daisy. The bells of Saint Mary of the Mountains and of the Presbyterian Church rung in salute. I leaned forward in the saddle, tapped easy on Daisy's right ear to guide her more to the middle of the road, and flashed by the office of the *Enterprise*.

Another quick look showed me that the Excelsior camel and another one had collided, knocking both riders sprawling into the street. The Virginia Hotel fella was gaining on me though, so I hunkered down close and urged Daisy on.

Up to now, things was according to plan, and I was already beginning to savor victory and my share of the winnings. But some of the local rowdies, aiming to add to the fun, had gotten to the livery stable hard by the fire station that marked the halfway point. They opened the corral gates that let out onto the road.

Blasting away with six-shooters and hoo-rahing and flapping their slouch hats, the boys drove ten head of mules and horses out into the path of the race. Daisy never slowed, but we spent a couple anxious minutes dodging amongst the bucking and plunging beasts.

When we circled the station and headed back up C Street, the confusion had grown even worse. By then the rest of the camels had reached the scene, and the mules were all in a frenzy. They set to kicking everything nearby, including some of the camels trying to come through.

I pulled Daisy to the side, finding myself clattering along the boardwalk in front of the Queen of Silver saloon instead of on the road. Onlookers scattered in all directions. A sign hanging over the planks almost knocked me out of the saddle, and when I righted myself, that's when I seen the child.

Up ahead, no more than a block in front of the rampaging mules and Daisy's flying hooves was a little boy. He had pulled loose from his mama and gotten between the packed spectators when they jumped back inside the buildings.

I could hear his mother screeching even above all the other noise. Being on the sidewalk, Daisy and me would miss him clean, but what about all them coming after?

Daisy was startled when I whapped her sharp on the jaw and turned her between two hitching rails. We spun round in the middle of the street, with her bawling and pitching like a ship in a hurricane. We was crossways to the stampede, twenty yards upstream from the herd with just a few feet separating us from the child.

I jumped from the saddle, caught my foot in the frame, and landed on my face in the road. Struggling up, I barely had time to grab the little boy to me and stagger back to huddle in the shelter of Daisy's bulk. The flood of mules and other camels parted as around a rock and raced by.

Giving the child back to its mother, I limped back to the finish line to apologize to Sam and the others. I had lost the race and with it all their money and my chance to get ahead on Lark's redemption.

Sam and Truro met me at the top of the hill. "It's terrible! Terrible!" Sam said.

"I know," I agreed, "but I'll make it up to you somehow. You and Truro and Kettle Belly."

"No, no!" They both yelled at once.

"Kettle Belly is dead!"

"He was knifed behind the grandstand!"

The murder of Kettle Belly Brown caused almost no stir at all in the lawless life of Virginia City. When robbery, beatings, and even killings happened daily, the hearts of the people was hardened unless it touched them close. For Sam and me and Truro, his death filled us with both sorrow and guilt, because we had been so close by and yet unable to help.

Lark knowed how hurting I was. Once, passing near me on the street, she said no word but pretended to stumble so's I could catch her. She murmured thanks and passed on, but in the brief touch passed me a note. It said she was praying for me and that I should be extra on my guard. But against what, she did not say.

And all the while my brain spinned out tale after tale of who done it and why. It was said to be robbery, since Kettle Belly had no cash nor watch on him when found, but I knowed that weren't really the cause. His death was linked to a war and other killings on the other side of the continent. There was at least one other who knowed the truth as well: the killer.

As hard as it may seem, life still went on after Kettle Belly's murder. More grim and silent than before, I drew back into myself and tried to give over to the work, as a way of getting on with my life.

The Mexican Mine was one of the richest diggings on the lode. Some of its ore assayed out at over one hundred fifty dollars to the ton. What that meant to us miners was that the money was there for improvements, to take the work deeper, further, and grander.

Even while I was following the drift at six hundred feet, digging was going on to deepen the shaft to close to a thousand feet straight down. What followed was a new tunnel at eight hundred feet, hitting the vein that much lower. It never failed to prove out that the deeper on the lode a mine went, the richer the ore.

The other thing that was always true is that deeper works meant more water flooding in, hotter conditions and greater danger for the miners. As the fastest working crew in the Mexican, Mackay's group—including me and Truro—moved down to the new level.

I seen Ward at least twice every day, at the beginning and ending of the shift, and sometimes during the workday when he come round to inspect. He didn't never recognize me as the young slave from New Orleans, not growed up and amongst a hundred other men, but once or twice I thought he looked at me funny, as if trying to place me. I figured to stay clear of trouble with him by working as hard as always and keeping my head down when he passed by.

My plan worked well, until the day come when we was drilling on the main face at the eight-hundred-foot level. Because of the slant to the vein of silver, the new works had yet to cut into the lode. Tons of worthless rubble had to be carted off before the tunnel again reached pay dirt. Ward give the order to cut straight ahead at full speed, drilling, blasting, and hauling out.

Now on that particular day, I was hammering and Truro holding the drill, same as always. The little tommyknocker doll set by our feet. We cut the first three of the blasting holes, but when Truro pulled out the bit to set up for the fourth hole I heard him say, "The devil!"

"What is it?" I asked.

"Take down the candle," he requested, "and hold it where I can study the bit." When I done what he asked, we seen that the last six inches of the drill was wet. "Go get Mackay," he said. "We'd best be testing this before we blast."

Water in the mines was often found in pockets, like bubbles trapped in the rock. Most times it could be drained away into the sump at the bottom of the hoisting shaft and then pumped out.

But sometimes the pocket would be immense in size and holding terrific pressure. Blowing it open could flood the tunnel with boiling water and steam. Sometimes the liquid was poison, blinding men it touched, or even killing them.

When such a pocket was suspected, work was stopped until test holes, deeper than the blasting holes, was drilled into the rock face to tap the pocket. Then it could be safely drained and the pressure released before the drilling and blasting continued.

John Mackay, being the crew boss of our level, understood immediate what Truro was saying and agreed to stop work on the drift. He sent for the extra long drill, the one as had to be carried by two men instead of just one. Truro was one of the men and a Swede name of Borger was the other. I was picked to do the driving, which Mackay said was to be done just above the floor level.

When the long bit was fetched, Ward happened to be standing near the rigging loft and he come along to see why it was wanted. When Mackay told Ward what was going on, Boss Ward had a fit. "I tole you to go ahead full speed with this here drift," he yelled. "Now you go and do the opposite! That drill ain't wet! Why, I spit more'n that! Get on with yer blastin'!"

Mackay protested that it weren't safe, and then Ward really got riled. He swung that short steel bar around and hit the wall of the tunnel, throwing sparks. Then he cursed and said if he had to say it again, he'd fire the whole level and get men who would take orders.

Real soft, Mackay said for us to go back to work, drilling the blasting holes. Him and the Swede went back to work on a crosscut to the main drift, around a corner from Truro and me. Ward stayed and watched us work 'til he seen that we wasn't going to slack off, then he went on up the way.

Truro and me finished the drilling, packed the powder and the rock dust into them holes, and strung the fuses from the blasting caps. Then we went into the other chamber and told Mackay we was ready to blast. He said that after we lit the fuse, we would all go up the hoist to the next level, instead of just staying in the crosscut, so as to be good and safe. Him and the Swede and the others working at that level headed on up. Truro and me was to follow soon as the fuse was burning.

When the level was clear, we set the fire to the cord, grabbed our candles and the tommyknocker, and then we run like crazy for the lift. It weren't there! "What can Mackay be thinking?" Truro said. "Ring for it, Jim."

I give the signal to lower the car, but nothing happened. Twice more I done it, and still no motion in the shaft to show that the cage was coming. "Quick," I said. "We'd best get around in the crosscut, so as to be out of the way of the blast."

No sooner had we reached the corner of the side passage than the charges exploded! Blasting rock sounds like a cannon going off, but the first noise was followed by more of a deep rumble in the earth. There was rush of air into the crosscut as the blast pushed a breeze out ahead of it. The lanterns and candles all blew out. That was not unusual, and I was already fumbling in my pocket for matches. My ears popped and then rung like bells, but everything seemed normal. I could hear the sound of boulders being rolled along the main drift and smaller chunks bouncing off ceiling and walls, but over that was a high-pitched hissing sound, like a locomotive pulling into a station.

I struck a match, but before I could relight the candle, around the corner of the chamber come a boiling cloud of steam! Truro was closer to the entrance than me, and he caught the first blast square in the face and give a scream. I flung up my arms across my eyes, and felt the rush of burning vapor scorch my ears and naked chest.

The match blowed out again, of course. "Come on," I said. "Back to the hoisting shaft."

The rumble and the hiss was followed by something even more scary—the crash and gurgle of a mighty stream of water. "Wait!" I hollered, "Keep back!"

I could not see it, but I could hear a rushing wave course down the main drift. If we had stepped out right then, we would have been in its path. As it was, a bubbling torrent swept along the tunnel and plunged in an underground waterfall over the edge of the shaft. A smaller wave bounced into our chamber, swirling around our ankles and making us jump from one foot to the other.

"Jim!" Truro shouted back. "Help me!"

He was mad with the pain. His eyelids was burnt and his whole face blistered. In the pitch black I couldn't see no more than him, but I weren't panicked, at least not yet.

"This way," I said, like it was clear to me. I grabbed on

to his arm and pulled him out into the drift. We coughed and gagged from the sulfur smell in the steam, and splashed through scorching pools that even after the first wave passed was again several inches deep and rising.

The next danger was that we would overrun the drift and fall two hundred feet down the shaft. Then we would be torn to flinders by the rocks and scalded to death in the sump.

My one hand locked on Truro's wrist and my other feeling the wall ahead of us, we scuttled sideways along the tunnel. At one point I slipped and fell down, dragging Truro with me. As my hand plunged into the hot water, it clenched tight of itself and brought up a lump of rubble from the floor.

The cascade dumping off the lip of the shaft warned me we was close. I could hear it pouring over the rim. Then a light appeared ahead. The cage dropped down into sight with Mackay aboard. He slipped his arms under Truro's and dragged him into the lift, then turned back to swing me in. Then up we soared, toward light and air.

"What happened?" I gasped out. "Where was the car?"

"Ward," Mackay said. "He found us on the level above and said we were wasting time again coming that far away from the charge. He wouldn't let me send the cage down for you; said you'd be all right in the crosscut." Mackay shook his head, looking at our blisters and Truro's swoll-shut eyes.

I forced my hand to unclench. The lump I had picked up still had its matchhead eyes, but the rest of the tommy-knocker's body was gone, busted to pieces and washed away.

Chapter 13

It took some time for my hands to heal up enough from the burns for me to swing a hammer again. The blistered places on my head and chest was sore, but didn't slow me none. Truro was worse off than me; his eyes was wrapped in bandages, and while the doc said he would not lose his sight, it would be a time before he could go back down in the mines.

Ward never admitted no wrongdoing; said it was an accident. And who was going to risk their own job arguing with him? Mackay did stand up for me in one respect, though. Since I couldn't work the double jack, Boss Ward was actually fixing to lay me off. Mackay stood right up to him about that, and told him that he would keep me on as a watchman 'til I healed up.

A watchman in the diggings is kind of a free-roaming spirit. The job is to keep an eye out for fire, for timbers that need shored up, for cables that need replaced, and so forth. Since he's not part of a regular crew, the watchman is also supposed to spy for the mining concern, keeping track of supplies and seeing to it that nobody steals company property. As such, he is not liked by the other miners, since he can turn them in for smoking and other forbidden practices. But because I were only fixing to do the work temporary, I didn't figure to have no trouble of that kind.

Sam reported the accident in the Mexican Mine. Even wrote me up as a hero for dragging Truro out of the drift. "Sam," I said, "there weren't nothing special about what I done. Truro or any of the others would have done the same for me. 'Sides, I was saving my own skin at the same time."

"Give it up, Jim," he replied. "This territory has precious few heroes to brag about, and, for the moment, you are one. Might as well enjoy it." Funny thing was, most folks showed their appreciation by stopping me on the street and offering to buy me a drink, which of course I had to decline anyway.

I might have got even more attention if it were not for the new fuss with the Washoe Indians. It seems that some miners had gone to chopping firewood. Now this weren't ordinarily no cause for discussion, but it seems this time they took it into their heads to cut piñon trees.

Sam said that was right foolish because everyone knowed that pine nut trees was too full of sap to burn, and that the Indians needed the nut trees for food. He even wrote a column laying out all this information for the uninformed public.

Old Winnemucca and Numaga, his son, made a trip to Carson to ask Governor Nye to stop the tree cutting. Nye couldn't do nothing hisself, so he sent the Indians over to Fort Churchill to ask the army for help. This is like killing a gopher by burying him alive; it sounds workmanlike, but it don't accomplish nothing. The army was not about to defend the Indians that they was there to defend against.

"Besides," Sam explained to me and in the paper, "more than that, the tree cutters are all Copperheads, led in fact by Bill Mayfield. Captain Moore will not provoke the rebels into a general uprising by arresting Mayfield and his crew. Not for doing something that only Indians care about."

So nothing but a lot of talk got done, but it occupied a mess of space in the newspaper. Sam said it made his job right easy.

———◆◆◆◆———

The worst thing about watchman duty in the Mexican Mine was the hours. Miners worked eight-hour shifts and there was three shifts each day: seven in the morning 'til three in the afternoon, three 'til eleven at night and "grave-yard" from evening 'til morning. Everybody got to be above ground during some part of daylight.

But the watchman's job, not involving swinging hammer or pick, not loading ore cars, was considered light work. There were only two shifts a day, from six in the morning 'til six at night, and the other the reverse of that.

Them hours meant that even though the days was at the longest of the year, since I had the daytime spell, I barely glimpsed the sun at all. It was right depressing to spend all my work time in the gloom of the pit, and when I come up to find gloom above as well.

Couple that with the fact that watchmen work alone and the darkness was inside of me as well as out. I had lots of time to reflect on Lark and our future together, which now seemed not even bright enough to be called uncertain. I brooded as I done my job, kind of chewing on my thoughts with half my mind.

One day Mackay sent me down in the secondary shaft of the Mexican Mine, to a platform at the one-hundred foot level. This passage had earlier been used for ventilation and to haul up ore. As the hoist brought up rock from below, it was dumped automatic by a device at the landing, spilling the contents of the bucket into cars. At the time of my arrival there, the station was not in use because that shaft was waiting its turn to be deepened. It was supposed to operate again soon, to join in the development of the lower reaches, and that is the task that took me there.

My job on that particular day was to inspect the machinery at the platform, to see what might need replacing. I checked the hopper and the cables, the mechanism of the dumper, and the bracing.

The inclined tunnel down which the ore slides after being dumped is called a winze. It slanted down away from the station to another drift where the tracks for the ore cars set. Now Mackay had not asked me to check the winze or the rails below, but I figured to save myself a return trip and so took my lantern and started down the incline.

Intermediate between the landing and the drift was a disused crosscut that connected with another mine. This weren't unusual; most of the mines bumped into their neighbors underground. Some even shared shafts or main drifts. The works of the Mexican intersected those of the Union Consolidated at this point.

But at that shallow a spot, none of the tunnels in the next-door mine was being used and it was all deserted. It was while passing the opening to the crosscut that I heard the clanking sound of metal on metal coming from the darkness beyond.

Mines being what they are, some noises are natural and to be anticipated, like small chunks of rock that drop unexpected from the ceiling. The groaning song of the timbers, the drip of water, or even the scurry of rats is soon recognized and paid no heed. But the noise of steel meant tools, and tools meant men, where none was supposed to be.

I stopped by the cleft and paused to think. It weren't none of my business what might be happening in the Union Consolidated. On the other hand, if anyone had been stealing tools or supplies from either the Mexican or the Union, this deserted passage was a likely spot to keep the secret.

That nothing honest could be happening in the drift was shown as soon as I crossed the threshold. The floor was half choked with sticky porphyry clay. In some places on the lode, the vein of silver ore is surrounded by this clay, a kind of real thick mud. It stays put until tunnels or drifts cut out the solid rock that holds it prisoner, then it oozes out of its seams from the weight of the stone above. Like squeezing the custard out of an eclair, it seeps into open spaces and has to be dug out and carted off. If anyone were planning to make use of this drift for mining purposes, the very first thing they would have did is taken care of the clay.

And if that weren't enough evidence, when I stepped over a mound of porphyry further back in the passage, I seen the brand new print of a boot, plain as anything in the wet mud. Right then I shielded my lantern down to a small glowing circle to keep it from being so easy seen and I crept along quiet. It never occurred to me to go get help; being watchman was my job and nobody's else.

I held the lamp up to guide me and to inspect the tracks

left by the muddy boots. There was two sets of them, both small men to judge by the size of their prints, and they had walked along side-by-side. The glow also revealed to me the rundown state of the timbers and the vault of an upraise as I passed beneath it.

After going fifty yards or so, I could hear voices speaking in low tones, and I aimed to find out what the speakers was up to. If possible, I would creep close enough to learn their scheme and their identities. At least, such was my intent.

Abandoned mines is lonely places at any time, but when moisture is present, like with the oozing mud, they get down-right uncanny. The timbers, which in an operating portion of the works are seen after and replaced as needed, quickly become the haunt of weird fungus that grows on the wood.

When the light of a candle or lamp strikes such a coat-ing, it glows in fantastic shades of green and yellow or even orange. That was what happened around the next bend in the Union tunnel. When I turned the corner, I jumped back sudden, because right in front of me was a hideous, gleam-ing face, leering at me with its dark yellow mouth, and looking at me from coal-black eyes between orange pointed ears. I stumbled over to a loose stone, banging the lantern against the wall as I made to catch myself.

I knowed right away that the evil image weren't no de-mon but an illusion formed by some of that fungus on an upright timber. But in the sudden start it give me, the dam-age was already done; whoever was up ahead of me must have heard the noise. I caught the sound of a sudden ruckus. "Someone's there!" a voice shouted, and then there come the clatter of footsteps coming toward me.

The fact that they was approaching told me something

right away: they felt strong enough to deal with whoever had chanced upon them, rather than running the other way. So it seemed clear to me to take myself off instead of sticking around.

I blowed out the lantern and run back the way I had come. Getting rid of my light kept me from being spotted right off, but made it impossible for me to get away very fast. When the shine of another light reached the tunnel wall beside me, I knowed there was no chance of me getting back to the winze and clear, so I started looking for a place to hide.

I was right then in the passage with the upraise. An upraise is a vertical dig that climbs from a drift to tap an ore body overhead. In the dark, I could not see how far the upraise went, but I hoped that it were high enough to be above the glimmer of the lamp.

Climbing them slippery beams was tough. I hoisted myself up on the first timbering alright, but then I had to crouch on the very edge of the beam. I needed to get higher out of the passage, but to go further, I had to stand up sudden, with my boot toes on the very edge, and thrust my length upwards into the unseen.

My fingertips barely caught the next ledge, and I somehow lifted myself. My burnt hand was shrieking with the strain and I couldn't have gone no further.

Two men stormed into the cavern below and stopped directly beneath me. "There's no one here," said one. "And no one has gone out. Look, the only footprints in the clay are ours made coming in."

I thanked the Lord that fella didn't count them tracks too close.

"I 'spose it's nothing. We's just jumpy is all," the second man replied, and the voice was that of Boss Ward.

"Let me finish what I was saying," the first man instructed. I strained my eyes to see could I recognize him, but he wore a hat and from my angle there weren't no way to make out his features. His speech did have a familiar ring to it, but I concentrated on the words. "My girls tell me that the Union officers have gotten in a shipment of two hundred rifles from California. Besides that, they have confiscated eighty weapons more from the militia headquarters at Carson in order to keep them out of secesh hands." The speaker chuckled at that, like it was humorous someway.

"When do we move?" Ward asked.

"Right now. The first act of our little tragedy will put the Yankees in motion tonight. The whole territory will be ours inside a week."

"An' the nigger? He's still askin' questions about what happened to Kettle Belly. Shall I finish him off?"

"Leave it be. It's too late for him or anyone else to stop us now. We can deal with him after."

My arm muscles was in spasm from the awkward position, clinging to the wall like a lizard, so I was right glad when they concluded their walk and headed off out of the tunnel. I waited 'til they went clean back into the Mexican drift and I heard the rattle of the hoist as they left the level. Then I finally eased myself down to the floor of the drift again, dropping the last six feet with a crash.

My mind was a whirl. "My girls," the fella said. Ryeman! What was Lark caught up in? That they were Copperheads bent on mischief was obvious. But what was their scheme and who should I warn? Who would take my word against Boss Ward's? These were all things I needed to know, and from the sound of things, time was short.

I did not know where to turn. I could not find Truro. And Lark? I was scared to see her. For one, it might put her in danger. Nagging at me was the thought that she was mixed up in it someway.

Sam was the only one I could count on, and he was the only one I could tell what I seen. Soon as my shift was over, I located him in his "office" in the Delta Saloon. He was up at the bar, bending the elbow with a bunch of his newspaper cronies. It was clear that some kind of celebration was going on.

"Sam," I said at once. "I gotta talk to you."

He acted real glad to see me. "Jim! Finally left the world of moles behind, have you? Come on, break your rule this once and have a drink."

"No, thanks," I said. "Anyways, I needs to see you. It's important."

"Why, so is this occasion." He waved two fingers to the barkeep the way he always done when he was buying drinks for hisself and a friend. "Mark twain," he called out, telling the barkeep to add two more to his tab. "You have to join me this once," he insisted. "I've been promoted. Joe is leaving Virginia for some business in San Francisco, and I'm to be editor in his absence." He said this last sentence real loud, as if all the folks in the saloon hadn't heard it twenty times already. But he was buying the liquor, so they give him a hurrah again anyway, to which he bowed.

I caught his elbow midbow and dragged him off of center stage and over to a corner table. I had first planned to talk with him outside, somewheres private, but with all the commotion in the Delta, we was in less danger of being overheard right there.

Sam was still smiling and waving to his crowd when I got right in his face. "Listen!" I hissed. "This is serious."

He swallowed twice and pursed his lips, and his head bounced a little as he tried to focus his eyes. It come to me that if this celebration had been running for very long, he would be worse than useless. I had to try anyway. "Hear this," I said. "I have got wind of a rebel plot, right here in Virginia City."

"A rebel plot!" he said at high volume, half standing up from his chair.

"Shhhh!" I said. "Don't talk, just listen. Ryeman is in it and so is Boss Ward. They plan to steal weapons from Fort Churchill. They say they have a scheme to take care of the soldiers. We gotta stop 'em."

Sam thought a minute, suddenly serious and blinking like a goggle-eyed owl. "You're right. We'll go together, you and me, to see Captain Moore. We'll warn him. He can arrest those two and lean on them 'til he finds out the rest. We'll go tomorrow."

"No," I said. "Tonight."

Chapter 14

The quickest route from Virginia City to Fort Churchill lay down the winding trail that went by way of Six Mile Canyon. Most of the freight and the travelers for the Comstock used Gold Canyon, further to the west, so Sam and I had the road all to ourselves. It was late to be starting on the trip to the army post, but no help for it.

The slope from town to the valley of the Carson River was steep. The looming bulk of Mount Davidson stayed spiked on the horizon behind, but the twinkling lights of the Comstock got quick swallowed up. And, all too soon, the twisting road dropped behind the cone-shaped mound called the Sugarloaf, and the shadows within the arroyo was very deep indeed.

Down below Flowery Peak, there was a trail that turned off of the Six Mile Canyon route to a small trading post. A battered wooden sign read DRINKS AND VITTELS. A hot east wind swirled the dust and moaned down the canyon. All at once our horses stopped all of themselves, and stood with their ears pricked forward, in the direction of the side path. Slower than our mounts, Sam and me picked up the clatter of hooves.

Then a horse and rider busted out of the dark ahead of us and come down the road at a gallop. Sam and I barely had time to rein apart before the unknown horseman split between us, so close that his stirrup touched mine. "Halloa," I hollered. "What's the trouble?" But the strange figure answered not a word. The echoing hoofbeats bounced off the rocks before fading into the whining of the wind.

"Who or what was that?" Sam said. "Could you see his face?"

But the collar of the rider's pitch-black duster was pulled up close and his floppy-brimmed hat tied down with a bandana. I could not even make out that he had a face, much less remark his features. "No," I said. "But nobody rides in that big a rush unless there's calamity. Come on!" I didn't give Sam no choice but put the spurs to my livery nag, and on toward the trading post we charged.

There was no light up ahead and nothing to show where the promised food and drink could be found. We located the saloon only by spotting a darker mass against a black cliff side. The door stood partly open. A faint, rust-colored glow from within showed that there had been a fire on the hearth, but it was burning mighty low. "This don't look good, Sam," I said. "Did you bring your pistol with you?"

He made no reply, but fumbled under his jacket and I took the action for a yes. Whilst I dismounted and walked cautious up to the doorway, Sam kept his horse in motion, spinning around like to watch every single direction at once.

"Anybody there?" I called. I crept up on the entry from the side, my heart pounding in my ears. I had no weapon at all, and as I come closer up to the door, I seen what I took to be a piece of stovewood laying on the threshold. Stretching out my reach, I stooped to pick it up.

It was a man's arm! His dark blanket coat sleeve I had mistook for a tree branch. "Sam!" I shouted. "Come here, quick!" The body lay face down in the opening, and it didn't take no genius to know he was dead.

Inside the post, which was no more than a single-room cabin with a wooden counter running across the far end, there was another dead man. By the poor light from the fire, I seen him lying just below the edge of the counter.

I found the stub of a candle and lit it, while Sam hovered outside the door, muttering curses under his breath. "What have we got here, Jim?" he asked in a gulping voice. "A double murder?"

"Looks like it," I said. "This fella," I added, pointing with my boot toe, "was likely the owner of this place." I showed Sam the greasy apron knotted around the man's neck. "Looks like someone come to rob him."

"Who's the other?" Sam hissed, stepping over the body in the entry with as long a stride as he could manage.

"Maybe one of the attackers, or maybe another victim." I dragged the body back inside the cabin and turned him over. It was an Indian. In fact, it was Echapa, the Washoe named Coyote that we had met up by the lake.

———— ◆•◆•◆ ————

It did not matter that the heavy dust obscured the road, or that we had to trust the good sense of those unfamiliar horses to keep us from flying off a cliff. With two dead bodies behind and the unknown phantom, possibly the killer, ahead, Sam and me hurtled down Six Mile Canyon like our lives depended on it.

As we galloped, I tried to piece together what we had found. Echapa had been gunned down. The hole just to the left of his breastbone had put paid to him. Fact is, he could not have moved an inch after that wound. How come we found him to be lying facedown in the doorway, a streak of blood stretching ten feet back to where his hatchet lay on the floor?

And what about the proprietor of the place? His skull had been split open, likely by that selfsame hand ax. But had he shot Echapa after receiving such a blow? It did not make sense.

On the face of it, it seemed plain enough. Echapa and perhaps other Indians had jumped the saloon keeper. The barkeep and Echapa had exchanged wounds, from which both died.

But Echapa was stone-cold dead—had been for some time—while the barkeep was still warm to the touch. I pondered that difference but come to no answers.

And over and under and intruding on all these thoughts was the puzzle of the lone rider. Who was he? He weren't no Indian, that much was plain. Could he have found the bodies and lit out for help, same as us? If so, he might have feared that we was the murderers returning. That would explain his desperate flight.

The only thing to be done was to tell Captain Moore and the army at Fort Churchill. For the time, even thoughts of rebel schemes was forgot.

We turned east when we hit the stage road, which was marked plain. Following the curve of the river for another five miles, the lights of Bucklands and the fort come into view.

We rode straight to the officers' quarters, a low adobe building on the north side of the compound. We wasn't challenged at all. Near as I could tell, the only sentry on duty was across the parade ground in front of the arsenal. There sure weren't no sense of urgency about the place.

As we drew rein in front of Captain Moore's quarters, Sam leaned over in his saddle and said to me, "Jim, I know Captain Moore. Orion introduced us. So I'll start off explaining, but you jump in anytime you see me leave out anything important."

We knocked on the door, and a burly Irish sergeant opened it. Sam explained who we was, asking to see the captain, and we was taken straight in.

Captain Moore was seated at a desk, writing by the light of an oil lamp. He glanced up and I seen him do a quick double look, almost like he couldn't believe what he saw. "Well, this is a surprise," he said. "Come in and sit down." He motioned to a pair of ladder-back chairs fronting his desk. "Sergeant," he went on, "would you please get Lieutenant Jewett and our other guest and return here at once? At once, you understand?" The sergeant give a quick snap of his head and a salute, then hustled out. "Now," Captain Moore said to us. "What can I do for you?"

"Captain," Sam said, "I hardly know where to begin. We actually came to warn you of a rebel plot to seize the arms stored here. But on the way, we discovered a murder, or perhaps it's two murders."

At the word murder, the captain stood up and drew his sidearm, a Colt army revolver. He didn't exactly point it at us, but he didn't lay it down either. "Perhaps you'd better tell me everything," he said. There was a cold edge to his words, and I begun to feel right uneasy.

"It was at the old Six Mile Canyon trading post," Sam begun. "One white man, perhaps the owner, has been killed. There is also a dead Indian, a Washoe named Coyote."

At that moment the door burst open again and the sergeant and the lieutenant fairly rushed in. They grabbed Sam and me by the arms, pinning us into our chairs. "What is this?" Sam sputtered. "What are you doing?"

The captain ignored him. "Come in, Mister Ryeman," he said to a figure lurking in the doorway. In strutted my worst enemy in the world, though he didn't know me from Adam: the man what held Mizz Lark's bond, and the chief of the rebel plot.

"Yes, that is the one," Ryeman said, pointing his finger at Sam. "I overheard him plotting with another secesh, but unfortunately, I did not recognize the other. It is just as I told you, Captain. The rebel gang are rousing the Indians to go on the warpath."

"But . . . but . . ." Sam stammered. "Jim here heard about a plot all right, but it isn't us. Tell them, Jim."

I craned my neck around to try and look into the eyes of the man known as Ryeman. "It was you," I said. "You're the fella I heard in the mine, scheming with Boss Ward. Captain, sir, you got this backwards."

To do him credit, Captain Moore looked right sharp at Ryeman when I said Ward's name, but Ryeman come back quick. "How clever," he said, "naming a man with well-known secesh sympathy in connection with me." He laughed then. "Come now, Captain! Are my papers in order or not?"

Moore looked a little embarrassed, and that was not good for Sam and me. "Mister Ryeman is a . . . works for the federal government. And you two are under arrest for treason, sedition, and murder."

"Murder?" Ryeman repeated.

The Captain explained what we had just reported, then said it was his belief that we had killed both men and cooked up the story to heat up the bad blood between the whites and the Indians.

Right then, something else clicked in my head. "I know where I seen you before," I said. "Back in Missouri. You changed your hair color and shaved off your beard, but your name is Grimes. I seen you when you was rounding up secesh militia for the fight at Springfield. You come to Pike's camp." Them last words slipped out before I seen what harm they could cause.

"There, you see, captain. They admit being in a rebel camp, with cutthroats of the worst sort. Just as I told you. I had already infiltrated the rebel ranks, and that's where I spotted these two. When I saw them again in Virginia City, I knew they were up to no good."

I seen what the game was then. Grimes was a Confederate spy, but he had somehow got papers to pass hisself off as a spy for the North. And we was being set to take the blame for his treason.

Sam was still unable to string two useful words together. "Captain," I said. "Does it make sense for me, a black man, to be helping the cause of the slavers?"

Captain Moore shot a look at Grimes again, but it was a nod of understanding and not questioning. I knowed that Grimes had planned for that objection too. "Some men will do anything for money," the captain said. "Lieutenant, take them to the guardhouse."

Sam finally found his voice. "Wait," he croaked. "You know my brother is the territorial secretary. Let me at least write him a note. He can straighten all this out, I'm sure."

Now I was not in the least bit sure that Orion could straighten out a twelve-inch ruler, but I blessed Sam for coming up with a delay anyhow.

We was both stood up, ready to be marched off to the hoosegow, but when the sergeant who was holding me seen that his commander was going to let Sam pen a letter, he just naturally relaxed. Being careful not to tip him off by tensing myself up, I let my shoulders sag.

Grimes smirked in the doorway, and the captain got paper and ink for Sam, who bent over the desk. The lieutenant stood behind the empty chair that had lately held Sam, and the sergeant was behind me.

I took a quick step to my right and back, turning toward the sergeant as I did so. I give him a shove that sent him sprawling into the lieutenant, and I whipped one chair after the both of them.

The captain reached for his pistol, and Sam wrestled with Moore, his two hands clamped on the officer's wrist. "Run, Jim," he yelled. "Get out of here! Go!"

As I started for the door, I seen Grimes reach under the skirt of the coat he wore, and knowed he was going for a gun. I threw myself at him full force, knocking him backwards through the doorway.

Grimes was smart. He grabbed onto my coat, knowing that all that was needful was for him to slow me down 'til the sergeant could recover and I would be caught.

So I didn't try to wrestle with him. I brought both my knees up to my middle, so when we landed it was with all my weight right on his chest. The air and the fight went out of him and he loosed his hold. I was up quick, and dashed off into the dark, snatching the reins of my horse as I went and doing a running mount from alongside.

I could hear everybody yelling at once, "Corporal of the Guard! Stop the prisoner. He's escaping. Shoot him!"

I didn't ever know if it was someone obeying that order, or the captain hisself who fired, but a bullet zinged past my right ear as I crouched low over the horse's neck.

More shots was fired after that, but no others come close to hitting me. I lit out across the desert, scarcely knowing where I was going, and only grateful for the dust storm that was hiding my tracks.

Chapter 15

The howl of the east wind was at full force, whipping my coat and stinging my face. Night and the high desert closed in around me, 'til I begun to feel as dark as being down in the mine. Sam was bound to get hanged as a spy, and the real spy was a snake being welcomed to the fireside. It looked hopeless.

Some vague notion of heading for Carson to find Orion kept me moving west. While I rode, I argued with myself that not even that would help. In the first place, Orion might be suspect too, and in the second, he would surely be watched, and here I was a fugitive from the same gallows as hung over his brother. But 'til something else presented itself, Orion was my only aim.

The dust storm turned the sage brush into heaps of piled-up sand. Distance was all distorted too. A hill that I fixed in my mind as a far bearing turned out to be a mound of weeds only a few yards off.

That was when I first realized that I was truly lost. I did not know where I was, nor how I had come there. I could not even retrace my own path, even if I had wanted to ride straight back to the fort and give myself up.

The wind had been steady out of the east. If I kept my back to the blow, I must surely run upon the stage road, or so I reasoned.

My eyes was so begrimed that it was difficult to raise the lids. Tied behind me on the saddle was a canteen. Getting off the horse, I used him as a windbreak to shelter myself from the gale whilst I splashed some water on my face.

I was also starving for food. I had not eaten since the noon meal because Sam and I left in such a hurry to reach the army post. I patted my pockets, but all I come up with was a little sack of them dried shrimp, left over from that day's lunch.

I left the packet inside my coat to keep it from blowing away, and drew out one piece at a time. The tiny bites of food give me a black humor: what if my last meal on earth should be what Truro called "husks of bugs"? It beat gnawing on sagebrush though, and I thought of Kettle Belly snatching up that woody turnip like it was a feast. Circumstances surely do change a man's perspective.

Crouching there, I debated whether to toss whole handfuls into my mouth and get substantial swallows, or stretch the morsels out a ways. The reins was laying across my shoulder and my back was to the horse, so I was totally unprepared when the nag give a snort and jerked his head around.

The reins trailed across the sand, and I dove for them but missed. My sudden spring put flight into the horse, and he slung his head around once more and took off trotting. "Stop, you misbegotten . . ." I yelled and I took out after him.

But he was moving with a purpose now, and kept out of my reach. His head was up and his ears pricked, like something called to him out of the bleakness. Had he scented another horse or the smell of hay in a stable, or was he headed clean back to Virginia City, following some bearing that only horses recognize?

I jumped over a dirt-clad lump that I took to be another bit of sage, but I was wrong. This mass of windblown grit hid a boulder, and there was a crevice on the other side that I had not seen before I leapt. My feet tangled up when I landed, and I sprawled on my face.

Though I snatched myself up quick as I could, the horse was gone, completely gone. I wiped the dust from my face, and took off running again, to follow his tracks. Then I seen it: a faint yellow light, low down on the horizon. Likely the horse had gone there for shelter or food.

Setting off towards the glow, I expected to come upon a prospector's camp, way out there in the desert and all. But when I got close enough, I seen the beehive-shaped mound of bark and earth. It was a Paiute campodie.

Stumbling straight into the cleared space in front of the hut, I spotted where my mount had gone. There was a makeshift corral, and my horse was craning his neck and turning his head sideways through the rails for a nip of bunch grass.

Now I did not know who or even what band these Indians was. Further, Sam and me had found Echapa killed dead but a few hours before, apparently in a fight with a settler. And if that was not enough, things was not exactly pleasant between the Indians and the whites over such matters as the pine nut trees. I wondered whether strange Indians would regard me as closer to white than they was. The best idea seemed to be to grab the trailing reins and ride off again.

But the scrawny donkey inside the corral settled that option. He give a loud snort and then a bray that would have waked the dead. From inside the campodie, three Indian braves emerged to see what the fuss was over. One had an old double-bladed ax and the other two was carrying knives. I was right surrounded, and they had not even been trying.

Not wanting to act suspicious or treacherous at all, I gave them a big howdy. Then I explained that my horse had run off and that I had followed him to their camp. I said if I could trouble them for directions, I would be on my way again.

It did not settle me that none of them responded. I did not know if they spoke no English, or if they was still sizing me up.

The question got decided when the one with the ax shook it at me and ordered, "Put up hands!" I did. I think I could have run off right then and got away, but they was between me and my horse and I would have been just as bad off.

The leader then gestured toward the entrance of the campodie. I had to duck to get through the low doorway, and once inside was backed up against the far wall separated from the entry by a low, smoldering fire.

The odor of that hut like to knocked me out. It was half full of sage smoke, and the other half was mixed of rancid fat, spoiled hides and none-too-clean bodies. There was no other of their kin there, just the three braves and me.

"I am a friend of Numaga," I said, trying hard to think of what might pass for a pleasantry. "You know him? Son of Old Winnemucca?"

The man with the ax sneered. "Old man and weak young man! Father and son more white than Indian."

"Well, I'm black," I said, pointing out the obvious.

"Enough talk!" said the leader. "You got money? Tobacco?"

I quick checked my pockets to see if I had anything to bargain with, but all I found was that half-eaten package of dried shrimp. "Nope," I said. "But if you'll let me go . . ."

All three laughed, and it was not a pleasant sound. Catching a stranger all alone out in their country made them ready to take out their anger without fear of reprisal. And I was that stranger. Were they going to kill me now?

The three exchanged a look, and give each other a sign of agreement. "Take off coat and boots," the leader ordered, shaking the ax at me. "We let you go, but we keep clothes and horse."

I took a real long time slipping my arm out of the sleeve, my brain racing all the time. The paper sack of shrimp crackled as I touched it, and I had a vision.

"You must not do this thing," I said in my deepest bass, singing-in-church voice. "I am a great sorcerer and I will turn you into . . . scorpions!"

"Huh," the leader snorted, trying to sound unconcerned. His two friends laughed also, but it weren't as hearty as before.

"You see this black skin?" I said. "I am a powerful

wizard that you das't not mess with. Watch this!" I reached in my pocket and pulled out a shrimp. I flipped my hand around so that dried thing fluttered in their faces like it was alive. "Who but a sorcerer has scorpions that live in his pockets?"

"Aiee," the youngest of the three said, looking ready to charge out the door. I was gaining on them.

"And watch this!" I commanded. I opened my mouth wide and tossed in the shrimp.

I knowed I had them on the run then, because they backed way up by the doorway to get as far from me as possible.

While their eyes was still on my crunching jaws, I snuck my hand in the sack of shrimp again and brought out a handful. "Maybe you want some?" I yelled and I threw the wriggling pieces.

In the flickery, smoky light, them things did appear just like scorpions. I almost couldn't blame them for screaming and clawing at theirselves to brush the crawly looking things off. The leader had the worst of it. Since he was closest, he got a half-dozen stuck in his hair.

They all three bolted and lit out in three different directions. "And don't come back or I'll do something even worse!" I hollered after them.

I knowed that my little trick would not keep them away forever, but I could now retrieve the horse and go on toward the west. It worked.

⸱⸱⸱

With the coming of morning, the force of the wind died. As I hoped, the gray dawn that lightened the sky above one set of peaks confirmed my travels, and I struck out toward the northwest. As the day broadened it weren't long before I struck the stage road and had my bearings again at last.

I dared not travel the road, for fear the army or some other might be set upon my track, but I could parallel it right easy and so kept my pace pretty steady. Twice I made out the form of travelers and hunkered down behind a sand dune 'til they had passed, but they was a good ways off and no danger to me at all.

Finally I was in sight of Carson and had something of a plan. Mostly what I had was a powerful hunger, since there had been nothing in the campodie that I felt inclined to eat and that handful of dried shrimp made far less impression on my belly than it had on the Paiutes.

Passing Carson City to the south, I circled round to approach the place as if I had only just come over the mountains from California. Then I found a spot to hole up 'til sundown when I crept up toward Orion's house.

Picketing my horse way out in the brush on the hillside, I slowly approached, bent low, until I reached a mound of rubble. That's when I discovered exactly what I had been expecting: namely two men guarding the house. They was nearer the building than I, talking in low voices. I gingerly raised my head up above the level of the heap of dirt 'til I could peer over it. The two watchers was holding conference beside the little shack called the necessary.

"I'll go back to where I can see up the street," one of them said, giving orders. "You hang here."

"If he'd been coming, he would of been here by now," the other replied. "He must of figgered we'd be watching the place and gone somewheres else."

"He ain't that smart," the first returned. "Unless he just hightailed it out of the territory altogether, he'll be along by-and-by. He's got nowheres else to go."

I swelled up some, hearing my intellect discounted so casual, but I deflated again quick at the other remark. They had me reckoned square to rights. Just then I wanted nothing so much in the whole world as to snatch up Lark over her protests and take us both far, far away.

And yet I knowed I could not do that; could not leave Sam to face hanging . . . could not let the rebels succeed in their plan. A steely resolve formed in the pit of my stomach, and I shook off my cowardly thoughts.

I snuck up toward the remaining guard, snaking from brush to brush, 'til nothing remained but ten yards of open ground. I bunched up my muscles the way I always done before swinging the sledge down in the mine, drew in breath and held it, and clenched my fists tight.

Something hit me in the back of the neck. It was just a pebble, but it might have been the whole of Mount Davidson for the way the impact shook me. My pent-up air went out like a shot, and I almost twisted my own head off cranking it around to see over my shoulder.

At first I couldn't make out nothing in the darkness. Then a second piece of gravel looped through the air to fall next to my right shoulder and I shifted my gaze some. Something small fluttered between two clumps of sage, like a blackbird flapping down near the ground. It was someone's hand, and they was gesturing for me to come back to where they was concealed.

Anyone with unfriendly intent would have nailed me with something stronger than a pebble, or raised the alarm if they was afraid I was armed. With the studied deliberation of a cat moving toward a mouse, I rotated my face back toward the guard to see if we had roused him.

There was no hurt done there. He was still pacing back and forth and only rarely stopped to study the black hillside. Keeping my gaze fixed on him, I slid backwards over the same ground I had just covered until a whole line of brush again obscured my position from the house.

Moments later another dark form detached itself from the chaparral and silently crossed to me. When it was right up next to me and the face full into mine, you could have knocked me over with a feather. It was Lark!

I plumb forgot myself, and had she not seen what was coming and put her hand acrost my mouth, I would've give us away for certain.

Keeping her palm over my lips, she brought her face right up next to my ear and whispered, "Jim, I've been so scared for you!" Her nearness and the scent of her perfume made my head spin. I stretched my arms to embrace her, but she shook her head and whispered to me again. "Can you get us both inside the house?"

I was totally fuddled at what was going on, but we couldn't stay where we was and discuss it. My instincts was to get Lark away somewheres safe, but I knowed she must have some mighty powerful reason to be there.

Giving a quick nod, I signed for her to follow me and back once more toward the house I slithered. I had no real plan except to rush the man and try to overpower him before he could use the six-shooter I was sure he carried. It had to be soon too, lest his companion come back. I felt a light tap on my heel that let me know Lark was right behind and ready same as me. But still I delayed, not daring to hope for any better chance, and yet waiting for some unknown signal.

It was fear for Lark's safety that made me hesitate, and that final pause was a godsend. In that span of moments, the sentry elected to light a cigarette, the lucifer match bright as a flare. It flashed to me that the lookout could not be holding a gun and even more, had blinded hisself as well.

I was already sprinting towards him before these thoughts had finished bubbling to the surface. I seen the startled look in the guard's eyes as he heard my running feet and caught the compounding mistake he made when he instinctively shook out the match before dropping it. That split second cost him the chance to draw his gun.

Even before the hand-rolled smoke dropped from his lips, and long before he had a chance to cry out, I was on him. My first punch went into his chest to silence him, and as he doubled up, choking and sputtering, I drove a second into his chin and straightened him up again. He went over backwards, his cigarette spinning through the air like a penny sparkler.

Lark raced past me toward the house. I paused just long enough to help myself to the guard's pistol, then pounded after her. I had my shoulder lowered, ready to bust in the door, but no need. Lark had it open and we both slipped in beside a startled Orion and Governor Nye.

———— ◦•◦•◦ ————

"Douse that light!" I yelled at Nye, same as if I was the governor instead of him. He blew out the oil lamp, and the room plunged into dark. "Get down on the floor and keep quiet! There's armed men watching the house," I said. "Keep Lark safe. I clobbered one of 'em and I'm gonna drag him in."

I heard Lark cry out, "No, Jim!" but I wanted lots of answers and the fella outside could supply some. Taking the Colt in my hand, I ducked low and eased open the door.

It was a good thing I bent down, because when the door opened a gunshot split the night and the slug splintered a length of doorjam off the frame, right level with where my chest would have been.

I snapped off a shot in the direction of the muzzle flash, then slammed the door shut and flung myself to the other side. Two more shots from outside ripped through the door itself. I rose up opposite to where I had just been and smashed the revolver into the window. I fired once, thumbed back the hammer and fired again, then dropped back to the floor. This time, instead of more gunfire, a cry of pain responded.

"Orion, you got a loaded gun in the house?" I asked. Being down to three shots without the means to reload did not set well with me. Orion made no reply, but presently a double-barreled shotgun slid over to me across the floor. I checked the hammers and found that it was indeed capped and ready.

There had been no further shots or sounds from outside, but even so I crossed to the opposite side of the door again and used the muzzle of the scattergun to gentle it open.

No shots responded. I poked the barrel out through the crack and waited. Still nothing. Gathering myself for a rush, I charged back out into the night, firing the last three bullets from the Colt Army left, right, and center. Throwing it down, I shifted the shotgun into position to do business and skidded to a stop beside the outhouse.

Dogs was barking all up and down the main street, but no more shots came. I hunted around to where I had knocked the man down. I found the remains of his cigarette makings, and right next to them a little puddle of blood. I scouted clear around the front but found no watcher there either.

"They're gone," I reported to the three folks back inside. "But if you're gonna light that lamp again, let's do our talking sitting on the floor."

"What is this all about?" Governor Nye demanded as Orion rekindled the light.

"Them fellas was secesh, looking for me," I said. "But as to what this is all about, I reckon it's for someone else to explain." I looked straight at Lark when I said this.

"He's in the middle of it now, Governor," my little innocent songbird said. "He needs to know."

Nye agreed. "Lark here is a federal agent. She has been working undercover, getting information on the activity of a rebel spy named Grimes. We know that they are behind the stage robberies, but we think there are bigger plans afoot."

"You don't know the half of it, Governor," I said, and I explained what I had overheard in the mine and what had happened to Sam and me since.

Orion laughed at the part about his brother being locked up at Fort Churchill. "Best place for him," he said. "Keep him safe for now."

"Yes, but Grimes was clear that something was about

to happen soon. Maybe even tonight! And now they know that I made it to you with my share of the news."

"I can confirm what he says, Governor," Lark added. "First of July, Grimes got word of a Confederate move north into Union territory. The plot here is timed to match."

"All right then," Nye allowed. "We need to warn Captain Moore at once!"

Orion and the governor studied me, same as Sam done when it come to anything involving physical labor. "I see how the wind blows," I said. "Just you write me out a letter to Captain Moore, Governor, so's he'll have something to read while he's fixing the noose around my neck!"

There was not enough time. Now that I had found my Lark, I had to be torn apart from her again right after.

"Now you know what I could not tell you befo'," she said. "Why I was so scared for you to come 'round me at all."

"You mean 'cause I would have give you away?" I teased.

"Jim Canfield!" she said, sounding right wrathy. "You don't think for one minute . . ."

She never did get to finish what she was going to tell me, because I grabbed her up in my arms and we clung together like the secesh and the war and the Comstock could all hike over Mount Davidson and leave us be.

At last I heaved a great sigh and turned her loose. "You know I gots to go see this through to the end, don't you gal?"

She nodded, twisting her hands together and running a

stream of tears that like to broke my heart. "Don't you get yourself killed," she insisted. "Or I'll never forgive you."

"Wipe your eyes," I said. "I'll come back for you. Besides, now that there ain't really a five-thousand-dollar contract to fill, we can take what I saved and get us a home of our own. I will never let you sing for nobody else long as we live."

She busted out crying all over again.

Chapter 16

Borrowing Governor Nye's black saddle mare, I set out toward Fort Churchill just as dawn was breaking. It were a most unpleasant feeling morning, grayly overcast but with no promise of rain to settle the dust. I rode east into a strange half-light, while black clouds raced toward me. The day got darker instead of lighter.

I knowed where I was headed and how I would get there, but had no idea what I was riding into. Nye seemed to think that once the word reached the rebel leaders about their plans being uncovered, they would hightail it out of those parts. I was not as certain. Seeing how casual they had killed Kettle Belly, and almost gone for me and Truro made me believe they would not panic so easy.

Not that my doubts had any effect on what I was called to do. Carrying the warning contained in the governor's note to Captain Moore and seeing Sam set free was my job, and I aimed to get it done and take myself back to Lark as quick as possible.

Whilst I rode, I thought about what I'd heard. If it was true that a big battle was under way in Pennsylvania somewheres, then this must be the great push by the Confederates aiming to bust the Union spirit. I called to mind the opinion of Horace Greeley that Sam had shared with me: a big victory back east and silver from Nevada Territory, and the Confederates could count on buying arms from England. If that happened, the North might be pushed into calling for a truce and ending the war.

The Union, the future of the country, was on a knife-edge, and one length of that shiny, sharp blade stuck up right between the hooves of the mare.

I rode past Bucklands at a high canter. The string of camels penned in the corral back of the stage stop looked like business was going as always. But even before I reached Fort Churchill, I knowed something was wrong. There were no companies of infantry drilling on the parade ground, no dragoons working with their horses, no sign of activity at all.

The first person I encountered was the same sergeant as had tried to capture me two days before. He come out of Captain Moore's office and seen me riding up. At first he give a wave, friendly like, then he seen who it was and whipped out his service revolver. Covering me with the muzzle pointed right at my brisket, he seemed astonished that I rode straight toward the porch. "You again?" he said. "What are you doing back? I figgered you to be halfway to Mexico by now."

"Nope," I said. "Got an important message for the captain from Governor Nye." I reached my hand inside my shirt and that Colt suddenly touched the end of my nose.

"Don't even move," the sergeant said through gritted

teeth. "I don't know what your game is. You may have put your head through the noose, but I'll blow it off before I'll let you get the drop on me."

"Easy, sergeant," I said, my hands straight up and still. "Just you grab the corner of that writing you see poking out."

Without moving the barrel of the pistol one inch, his left hand stretched out toward my blouse and two fingers snagged the message. "That's it," I said. "Pull it on out, it ain't going to bite you."

"What'd you say this was?"

"Message for the captain. Say, where is he, anyway? Where is everybody?"

"I ain't telling you nothing, you reb spy! Get down easy and step away from that horse!"

I did as I was told, then at a wave of the Colt, backed up into a corner of the porch whilst he unfolded the letter.

His eyebrows went up as he read the letter and he looked up at me over the top of it. "You know what this claims?"

"Yep," I agreed.

"How do I know it's genuine?"

"Well now, you don't. You go ahead and lock me up whilst you and the captain sort it out. Just alert the guard so's no rebs catch you by surprise."

The look of concern that passed over the sergeant's face did my feelings no good at all. "Captain ain't here. Message come at dawn that the Washoes attacked a stage between here and Williams. A massacre. Captain Moore ordered everybody to arms and off they went in pursuit."

"Everybody?"

"All three companies. Left me here to guard the prisoner and look after things. There's two sentries and two more men down sick and that's it."

"What was Captain Moore expecting, a thousand Indians on the warpath? Who brought the report?"

"I did," said the voice of Abner Grimes from the doorway.

———————

Grimes relieved the sergeant of his pistol and with the pair of us prisoners marching ahead, managed to take the two sentries unawares as well. He captured all four as easy as pie and now prodded us toward the guardhouse.

"You're crazy," the sergeant said. "The whole troop will be back soon as they find out it's a hoax. If you want to save your neck, you'd better take off now."

"I don't think so," Grimes chuckled. "See, there really was an attack and now some of my men are leading Captain Moore on a merry chase toward Utah Territory."

"What do you think you'll gain?" I said.

Grimes, like most sneaks and scoundrels when they have the upper hand, did not mind bragging on hisself. "To start with, we'll have that whole stack of Spencer repeating rifles from California and enough ammunition to outfit my whole regiment."

"So you and your traitors," the sergeant sneered, "can use 'em to kill squirrels when you go hide out up in the hills?"

"Hide out? No, no. My regiment is just waiting 'til I signal them to capture the fort. Then we will use the Spencers for a different purpose when Captain Moore returns."

The sergeant had been walking a little to one side of the rest of us, and perhaps his aim had been to distract Grimes with the talk. But the idea of his comrades riding right into a cold-blooded ambush pushed him over the edge. Giving a hoarse cry, he whirled around and jumped for the throat of the rebel spy.

The Colt in Grimes's hand blasted. I don't know whether he was just quick or if he set the sergeant up on purpose to make him try something, but he cooly shot the sergeant in the throat and dropped him in the dirt. Ignoring the man writhing at his feet, he waved his pistol at the rest of us and invited, "Anyone else care to try their luck?"

Nobody spoke and Grimes waved us on toward the guardhouse. "He'll bleed to death," I protested.

"Let him," Grimes said, "unless you want to join him."

The guardhouse at Fort Churchill was a simple, adobe block building that faced the parade ground on the far side of the compound. It had only two cells and both of them opened onto the open air, underneath a roof that gave some meager shelter to the guard's walk outside.

Even though the day had grown steadily darker from the ominous black clouds, up ahead I could see Sam. He grasped the bars of the window in the door of his cell, his face pressed up against the opening. "Hello, Sam," I called out. "Looks like we're going to be cooped up together for a spell. I hope you got your pipe, and tobacco enough for us both." I prayed he would catch my drift while there was still time.

"Us both?" he said in surprise. "You don't . . ."

"And matches and your tool for tamping," I added hastily.

I could see Sam look down and fumble with something, then hold up the round bowl of the meerschaum to the bars. "Got it right here," he said.

"I can hardly wait 'til we get inside," I said.

"Shut up and move faster," Grimes ordered. "This is no party."

Grimes ordered Sam to stand back from the door while he had me slide back the bolt on the latch. He motioned with the gun for the soldiers and me to get inside. I purposeful dawdled a mite to let the soldier boys get clear of the entry.

"Hurry up, nigger," Grimes said. "I've had enough trouble with you already. I'd as soon blast you as look at you."

"Me too," I said, flinging myself all of a sudden inside and behind the wall. "Now!" I yelled.

For a man who never hurried to do anything in his whole life, Sam acted right fast on that occasion. From holding his pipe up to his mouth casual, he whipped his hand forward like he was throwing a baseball, aiming that shiny yellow bulb at the feet of Grimes.

There was a roar as the blasting cap Sam had stuck into the bowl exploded, and pieces of stony meerschaum peppered the air like shrapnel from a six-pound cannon. Grimes screamed and clutched his face. He triggered off one round that struck the adobe and whined away harmless, then I was on him. I kicked his arm hard and the pistol flew from his hand. The left that I connected with his chin had more force behind it than was strictly necessary, but I were too impatient right then to hold back. Grimes lay sprawled across the walkway, blood streaming down his face from a dozen cuts.

"See to the sergeant," I yelled to the soldiers. "I'll take care of Grimes."

———◦•◦•◦———

I do not know what signal Grimes was supposed to give to launch the attack, but the explosion of the meerschaum grenade served the purpose. With rebel yells and pistol shots, a troop of horsemen about twenty-five in number swept out of a canyon about a half mile west of the fort.

There weren't no time for anything like strategy, just quick action to see to defense. "Barricade yourselves in the armory," I said to Sam and the two guards. "Hold them off as best you can."

"What about you?" Sam called out to me as I ran toward the governor's horse still tied to the post across the square.

"Got an idea," I hollered in return. "I'll be back!"

Sam and the others would have to fend for themselves, for as I vaulted into the saddle of the black, the front rank of the secesh boys spotted me and the chase was on. Three of them rebs peeled off after me, and the others took to circling and firing into the armory. Coming behind the horsemen were three empty wagons to haul off the plunder, and bringing up the rear, bouncing and jolting, was a small cannon. It didn't take no genius to figure out where Fremont's howitzer had wound up.

But that was all I had time to take in before I bent low over the mare's shoulder and laid on the quirt. I was never so glad of the use of any horse as in the mile or so that separated me from Bucklands station. That critter showed a turn of speed that served us well. A couple bullets whizzed past, but a quick glance over my shoulder showed we was pulling ahead and another minute brought us within sight of Bucklands. The three rebs changed their minds about me and doubled back toward the fort.

A stage was pulled up at the station, the driver setting on the box. It was Frank. "Rebs are attacking the fort and the boys need help," I yelled. Frank never argued nor questioned, but just bellowed for all real men to grab their guns and get out there on the double.

One of those that bailed out of the saloon was Truro. "Saints above!" he yelled. "Is it you, Jim? I thought you were killed for sure."

"Not yet," I called back, "but plenty of folks been trying. Pile as many as have rifles into the coach and head out . . . the war has come to Nevada, but I mean to head it off."

<hr/>

My return to Fort Churchill showed an amazing scene. At the center of the action but only dimly seen in the twilight at midday was the adobe block armory. Through narrow rifle slits designed for just such a purpose, Sam and the two guards was giving a good account of themselves, forcing the rebs to keep their distance. The secesh fellas fired into the building, but the main threat was at the front where they had planted the howitzer just opposite the lone entry. One poorly aimed round had already knocked a cornice off the building, and another had blowed a three-foot hole in the wall just left of the door.

The lives of those inside the blockhouse wasn't worth spit if the cannon continued in play, but so far Frank and Truro prevented it from being aimed better. Outside the circle of rebs, Frank whipped the stage back and forth past the rebel line, while Truro directed the rifle fire from inside the coach.

The short figure managing the cannon seen that he could not succeed less the stage were eliminated, so he ordered most of the attackers to mount up again and assault the coach. That was exactly what I was counting on.

When I come over the ridge nearest the fort, I rode Daisy, and I led a pack string of six more camels at the fastest rolling gallop ever seen. I kicked Daisy into a charge as down the slope we bowled, with me "hut-hutting" for all I was worth. The rest of the string ranged theirselves alongside as if they sudden figured it was a race.

My camel brigade struck the center of the reb line of cavalry, and every horse critter within a hundred yards went to bucking and plunging. Such a mess of hollering and cussing was never before heard on the planet. Fighting a battle and capturing the fort was altogether forgot; it was all those boys could do to hang on with both hands!

That little fella that had been the leader was none other than Boss Ward. His horse, a genuine Mexican plug, jumped straight up and come down with all four feet planted together. That landing must of drove Ward's tailbone clean up to his neck. Next bounce, he shot up in the air with both feet out of the stirrups.

Most of the rebel troopers was forcible dismounted by the time I made my second pass through the line with the camels. Then Frank whipped the stage across the field again, and Truro's boys winged a couple more of the secesh. The ones still more or less in their saddles lit out for the hills.

About that time, Sam and the two soldiers come flying

out of the blockhouse and seized the cannon from an astonished reb. Unlike the half-hearted men Ward and Grimes had recruited with promises of loot, the two Union soldiers knew how to handle that howitzer. They spun it around and brought it to bear on the only group of secesh that remained standing. One of the Union soldiers hollered out, "We loaded her with canister. If we fire at this range, there won't be enough of you left to bury!"

"Yeah," hollered Sam, real warlike. He shook his fist too.

That was the end of the battle of Fort Churchill. Frank swung once more around them rebels, dropping Truro's men off in a circle. The rebs throwed down their guns and raised their hands. At rifle point, facing a cannon loaded with grapeshot, and with their mounts still dancing like crazy critters, what else could they do?

Ward had finally bounced to a halt, but he had no intention of being caught. He spurred his horse toward the armory, intending to race back up into the canyon from which the attack had come. From the doorway of the block-house staggered the figure of Abner Grimes. He waved both arms and yelled for Ward to save him.

Boss Ward jerked his horse down to his haunches in front of the door and triggered off two shots that made Sam and the federal soldiers duck behind the cannon. I seen Ward reach down to give Grimes an arm up and seen Grimes yank Ward out of the saddle to the ground.

As Grimes jumped into Ward's place and spurred the horse, Ward run alongside tussling and pleading with Grimes not to leave him. The two had been comrades moments before, but now fought over the means of escape. A volley of shots rung out, from the soldiers and Truro's riflemen, and both Ward and Grimes hit the ground, stone dead.

We rounded up all the secesh and locked them in the guardhouse. All at once Sam yelled out that Mount Davidson was on fire. "The rebels have torched Virginia City!"

There was a tongue of flame, dark red, that streaked the sky in the black clouds swirling around the peak. "Can't be the town," I said. "It's too high on the mountain."

"But something is on fire up there," he insisted. "Look at the length of that flame shooting out!"

I had terrible misgivings to see the brilliant fire in the middle of the pitch-black clouds. I wondered what it could possibly mean; was it an evil omen of terrible import? I called to mind the danger the country was in. What if our little victory in Nevada Territory had come too late?

A shaft of sunlight busted through the clouds right then, straight to the peak as if aimed at the pinnacle of Mount Davidson. There, revealed to all in its true nature, was the reality of the flame on the mountain: it was the giant red, white, and blue banner . . . Old Glory . . . still waving, proud and free.

It wasn't 'til a whole day later that the telegraph brung the news. The Yankee boys had won a bloody and terrible battle at a little town called Gettysburg. General Robert E. Lee was whupped and turned his troops back toward the South. The worst danger to the Union was over.

That was the end of that rebel threat to the silver mines in Nevada Territory. There was still those who favored the

South, but they was more quiet and Fort Churchill more alert after July the Fourth, 1863.

With Grimes and Ward both dead, there weren't no leaders for the secesh. Bill Mayfield was the one who killed the saloon keeper and Echapa, meaning to stir up the Indian troubles. But others in the gang turned rat on him and he fled to Mexico.

Grimes was the one who killed Kettle Belly's family back in the border wars, and it was the voice of Grimes that Kettle Belly recognized on the day of the camel race. Course, that discovery ended up costing Kettle Belly his life as well. That I was connected with Kettle Belly is what put Ward on my track and what almost got Truro and me killed in the mine. I don't believe Boss Ward ever did recognize me for the child he stole and sold back in '49.

I have often wondered why Sam did not write up this whole story hisself. When I asked him that once, he said his made-up stories was easier to swallow than the truth of this one, but that he would use bits and pieces of this tale in different yarns. And so he did.

EPILOGUE

The sun was setting behind the Sierras. The peaks south-west of Virginia City were outlined with a golden glow, while streaks of orange faded into pinks and purples in the gathering dusk.

Seth Townsend wiped his forehead and reached for the pitcher of tea. It was empty. This observation brought him to notice how late it had grown. Where had the hours gone?

"Sorry, Mister Canfield," he apologized. "I've taken up your whole day." Townsend looked at his watch. "And I've even missed all of the story about the train." Then he smiled; a slow grin crept across his features and was returned by the man seated in the porch rocker. "You are like . . ." he began, the he corrected himself. "You *are* a time machine. Could I borrow some of your pictures to run with the story? I promise to return them."

Jim Canfield stood up and despite his stooped shoulders and bowed knees, he moved with remarkable ease and sped through the screen door and into the house. He was back a moment later with an armload of fading prints. He passed several to Townsend—portraits of long-dead miners and views of buildings in Virginia City that had been swallowed up by fire fifty summers before. But one heavy silver frame he kept back in the crook of his arm.

"You can borrow any you like," Jim offered. "'Cept this one." Almost shyly, he turned the withheld photo so Townsend could see. It showed a proud muscular figure in tall boots and a shiny black suit, who could have been Jim Canfield's great-grandson. Next to the young man in the portrait was a woman dressed in white, her lace veil pulled back to outline a face that glowed with happiness. "This one," Jim Canfield said with a catch in his voice. "It's of Lark and me on our weddin' day. I cain't part with it for even one night."